GODS & MONSTERS

Book 7 of
THE WARDEN

FELICIA JEDLICKA

For those who would rather fight for their dreams than have them handed to them.

SISTER WITCHES
THE DEVIL'S SHADOW
THE DEVIL'S SOUL

DESTINY REJECTED
DESTINY RECLAIMED
DESTINY RAZED
DESTINY RESTORED

DÉJÀ VU

SAVE THE HUMANS

THE NECROMANCER'S CHILD

<u>THE NEBRASKA APOCALYPSE NOVELS</u>
CORN COWS AND THE APOCALYPSE
COW TIPPING AFTER THE APOCALYPSE
CORN HUSKING AFTER THE APOCALYPSE

<u>THE WARDEN SERIES</u>
SUCCESSORS
RIVALS
LOVERS AND LIARS
BAD BLOOD
TENANTS AND TYRANTS
THE RING BEARER
GODS AND MONSTERS
BEASTS AND BURDENS
MAGIC AND MAYHEM
FORK IN THE ROAD
DETAILS AND DEADLINES
*CURSES AND SACRIFICES**
*WITCHES AND WOLVES**
*SAINTS AND SERPENTS**
*ENEMIES AND ALLIES**

MARRIED TO DEATH*

GODS & MONSTERS

FELICIA JEDLICKA

"**M**OM." Cori could feel reality seeping back into her muscles, but not her mind. Before she could fathom what to say to her undead mother, Emily Reiger pulled her sackcloth towel off her shoulder and rushed to clean up the spill at Cori's feet.

"Corinthia Ellen, what is wrong with you? Nearly thirty years old and you still can't manage to keep from making a mess in my house."

While Emily mopped up the coffee, Cori looked to the calendar that always hung on the side of the fridge with red Xs on the past days. The date was right, but nothing else. Her mother had passed away some five years ago, just before she headed to college. Her aunt had supported her during that time, before she also passed away. Cancer had taken them both.

Cori looked around the kitchen. Everything was familiar, but with a few added features: small appliances, different dish towels, and the curtains over the sink had been exchanged for wood blinds. This was still her mother's home, the one she had lived in while finishing her secondary education.

"Corinthia, are you just going to stand there? Here, take this cup so I can get up." Cori took the mug and set it in the sink before helping her mother off the floor. "What is wrong with you?"

"I..." She wasn't sure how to answer that. It was clear that making her wish to "go back to *normal*" had returned her to her previous home with her mother, but what else had changed? What had happened to Ethan and the others?

There were too many questions that she wouldn't be getting answers for any time soon. Instead of dwelling on those mysteries, she focused on the moment and did something she hadn't been able to do for many years. She hugged her mother.

Cori could feel Emily accept the hug willingly, just as any mother would, but the intensity of the embrace made her uneasy. Emily soon pushed her away and pierced her with sky-blue eyes. For the first time, Cori noted the similarity between Efrat's eyes and her mother's. She cringed at the comparison and wondered how much of her trust in Efrat was born out of a misplaced reminder of her mother. Someone could write a thesis on that psychological conundrum.

"Corinthia, what is wrong? Are you okay?" Emily kept hold of her shoulders, squeezing just hard enough to demand the answer she sought.

Cori smiled and pushed her mom's frizzy waves back behind her ear. She was always thankful that she had inherited her mother's hair, minus the frizz. "I'm okay, but..." She wasn't sure honesty was going to be the best protocol, but this was her mother. If she couldn't tell her the truth, who could she tell?

Plus, it's not like they were near any asylums.

"Mom, something unusual has happened and I'm not sure how to tell you, but I have to."

"Oh, God, are you sick? Please tell me you didn't find a lump. That fucking cancer!"

Cori was taken aback by the cuss word from her mother, but she was certain if anyone deserved to curse about the disease, it was her. "No, Mom, not cancer."

"Oh, good. I don't wish to relive that disease a third time, certainly not through you." Emily kissed her on the cheek, no doubt leaving a smudge of coral pink lipstick. It wasn't the best color for her, but she insisted it was. "It was hard enough with my sister." Emily moved to the sink to continue her dishes.

"Mom, I'm not in the right place." Cori followed, picking up a towel to help dry.

"Oh, sweetheart, it's just a starter job. You can't expect to get a high-paying job straight out of school."

Cori sighed and shook her head. This would not be easy. She could just say that she made a wish and got thrown out of her own reality, but that would be like telling someone that dolphins weren't fish when they didn't understand the difference between lungs and gills. She needed to start simply.

"Mom, you're supposed to be dead." Perhaps that was too simple.

"I know, dear, and I thank God every day that I'm not. Are you ready for a scone? I think they've cooled enough."

"*I'm* ready for one," a deep voice bellowed from the hallway, preceding a tall, lanky, chocolate-haired man. His tie hung loosely around his neck, and three buttons on his white shirt were undone. He was handsome in a stately way. His face was all chin and forehead, and his frame all portrait and no profile. He had to be taller than Danato, which made him tower over Cori.

"Oh, Geoffrey, you are always ready for dessert," Emily chided him before dishing up one of her infamous scones for him.

When Geoffrey sidled up behind Cori and put his arm around her, she resisted the urge to shove him away. Instead, she checked his hand for a ring. He wasn't wearing one—but she, meanwhile, was still wearing all ten of hers, including her wedding ring. That didn't seem to make sense, since she wasn't wearing the same clothes.

Point, in fact; she was wearing a black, spaghetti-strapped, wide-leg jumper with high heels. Given that her male friend was wearing a suit, and her mother had on a rather nice violet dress, she wondered if this was a special occasion. She didn't like the sound of that. She was already in a bind, without more *special* to add to it.

"What about you, cupcake?" Geoffrey tugged her shoulder, pulling her against him so he could speak close to her ear. "Do you want to celebrate our engagement with dessert, or should we celebrate with our own dessert later?" He chuckled at the innuendo and Emily scoffed, but smiled warmly at him.

"Oh, you hold your tongue, Geoffrey. She's still mine until you can pry her out of my hands."

Geoffrey withdrew from Cori, offering her a reason to relax her tensed muscles. He moved to her mother and plucked up her hand. He withdrew the spatula she was holding and set it back on the platter. "Mrs. Reiger, you know if you don't let her go, I'll just have to take you both." He winked and kissed her hand.

"Oh, you rake," she teased, drawing her hand away, but Cori could see her blush. It was unusual to see her mother affected by a man. Granted, it was unusual to see her at all nowadays, but she wondered what she would think of Ethan. Would his reserved demeanor make her think he was cocky? Would his territorial nature cause her to assume he was controlling? She was certain Ethan couldn't charm his staunch mother like this man, but she would have enjoyed watching him try.

Geoffrey came back over and tried to kiss her, but she recoiled. He looked at her, baffled and a little hurt. She stepped away and tried to come up with an explanation, but she didn't really have one to offer. "Darling, I was only teasing."

Emily looked her over and turned back to Geoffrey. "I think the engagement is starting to settle in. She's already concerned about how much money her job is contributing."

He exhaled with exasperation. "I told you, if you want to continue to work when we have children, I'm more than happy to pay for a nanny."

Cori nodded, but part of her wanted to roll her eyes. Was this her life without the prison—married to the cliché charming businessman that for all his modern ideals still didn't understand the real world, because he had just enough wealth to avoid it? It was her ideal *normal* life, or at least it had been three years ago. Now it just seemed mundane.

"It was really good seeing you again, Mom," Cori said, biting her lips hard so she didn't choke up.

"We saw each other yesterday. Where's your marbles, girl?" Emily said, gathering up more scones to take to the dining room.

"I wish to undo my wish," Cori said to the heavens—or, from this perspective, to the ceiling. She anticipated a warping of images, maybe even to black out, but nothing happened.

"What are you saying?" Geoffrey said, wide-eyed. "Are you saying you don't want to marry me?"

"No!" Emily jumped in before Cori could answer. "She doesn't mean that. Do you, Corinthia?" Her eyes showed as much anger as expectation.

"No, that's not what I meant. I was just..." *Trying to talk to my genie.* "Listen, Geoffrey, I assume you were planning on taking me home tonight."

"Yeah, of course, unless you'd rather go to your flat?" He sounded so accommodating. Had she not already been married, she might have considered him charming, even if he was a walking high-rise.

"Actually, I'd prefer to hang around here. I really need to speak with my mother. You understand, right?"

"Oh," he said, as if he had just figured out what was really going on. "Girl talk?" He winked.

"Something like that." She smiled to offer him some kindness. She may not have intended to stay in this reality, but there was no reason to get tangled in the details.

"Say no more," he said and embraced her. "I will leave you two be, but tomorrow I am taking you shopping for a ring. Maybe at last we can get those wretched things off you." Cori looked down at her rings, once again surprised that they were still there despite everything else being different.

"I..." Cori looked up to respond to Geoffrey, but he kissed her. She played her part and received the kiss. It was too wet for a goodbye kiss, and too soft for a meaningfully heated kiss, though she might have been biased since she preferred Ethan's lips to any other man's.

He pulled away, and the goodbyes went on longer than necessary. Emily insisted on packing a scone for Geoffrey to take. She seemed baffled by the change of plans, but didn't waffle at having Cori stay longer. When Geoffrey was finally out the door, Emily headed into the dining room to have her coffee and dessert. Cori followed and nibbled on a bit of scone before proceeding with the nasty business of the truth.

Emily sensed the shift in her demeanor and started to scowl at her. "Young lady, I don't know what has gotten into you. Suddenly, after a beautiful proposal, you shrink away from a man that is so devoted to you."

"Mother," Cori interrupted. "I need you to shut up."

"I will not..."

"Mother!" Cori snapped, and Emily remained silent behind her angry shock. "I know you have questions, but they are all irrelevant. I'm going to tell you everything, after which I will leave. I need to go someplace where I can get help, but I'm afraid that means leaving you behind, perhaps forever."

"Corinthia..."

"Mom, I just need you to listen. I've been without you for a long time, and I want to tell you what I've been doing. I don't have time for disbelief or concern or even opinion. I'm going to give you the rough cut of my life over the last five years, and at the end I'm going to fetch a cab and go to the train station, so it's very important to me that you listen, because I may not get a chance like this again." Cori's eyes watered, but she cleared her throat and demanded of herself not to let emotion ruin this opportunity to tell her mother about her life.

Cori started her tale of woe, explaining that in her version of events, Emily didn't survive the cancer. Cori's mother looked a little pale upon hearing that, but didn't interrupt. When the story turned to the strange underworld of Danato's prison, Cori recognized the askance look in her eyes. It wasn't until Cori discussed Ethan that something changed in her mother. Perhaps it was the way Cori described him, or maybe her mother just recognized love, but Emily was smiling.

Even with the basics, Cori still needed to explain a little about the elementals and the magic lamp. Before she knew it, over two hours had passed and her mother was wrapped in the story as if bound by a good book.

Perhaps even a great book.

"As happy as I am to see you, and as much as I want to stay here with you," Cori said, feeling her eyes well with tears that she couldn't stave off any longer, "I have to find my husband. I have to figure out how to get back to where I was. I don't know how much I've changed things."

Emily pushed away her scone, which had long since cooled on her plate. "I'm so sorry."

Cori furrowed her brow. "For what?"

"For letting the damned cancer win!" she said, crossing her arms.

"Mom!" Cori laughed at her mother's ability to accept her story as truth, despite the insanity of it. "You fought a good fight. I know you tried, but it was just too much."

"Still, I should have had them chop off my breasts at the first sign. Foolish pride."

"It wouldn't have helped. It was too far along by the time we found out." Cori wiped away another row of tears and reached out, squeezing her mother's hand. "Mom, I don't blame you. I'm not trying to make you feel bad. I'm trying to tell you that... I'm happy. As crazy a world as I just described, I love it. I only wish... no, I don't wish, but it would have been nice if you could have met Ethan."

"If he loves you as much as you claim, then I'm sure I would have loved him."

Cori moved around the table and hugged her. Emily held her for a long time before they separated. Cori could see the pain in her eyes. They both had the same thought in mind. *Just stay.* If only it were that simple. As much as Cori loved her mother, in making her wish come true, she had undone everything she had accomplished in the past two years. She wanted to be with her mother, but she also wanted to be with Ethan.

"A mother doesn't like letting go of her little one," Emily said, breaking the silent debate. "But you have been a daughter long enough. It's time for you to be a wife and mother. God willing, you will even have time in your life to be a grandmother."

Cori smiled. She couldn't imagine being a mother, let alone a grandmother. "I love you, Mom."

"I love you too. I hope I wake up from this dreadful nightmare and find that this was all a dream, but if I don't..." Emily's eyes finally welled with tears, breaking the controlled façade that Cori hadn't inherited. "You know this." Her finger flew in Cori's face with as much threat as a nun's ruler prepared to whack naughty fingers. "If you come up to heaven before your time, I will kick your butt straight back down to this Earth." Cori laughed, despite the river of tears that were officially irrepressible. "You take care of yourself."

"I'll try."

"You will," Emily scolded.

Cori nodded. "I will."

As with any family reunion, the goodbyes lasted forever. The conversation jumped to different topics as they avoided the inevitable. They both went back for more scones and laughed about the good times before cancer and funerals. For a while, things really were *back to normal*, even if it was the wrong normal.

Emily drove Cori to the station instead of letting a cab take her. It was early morning by the time they made it. The last call to the train was the only thing strong enough to pull Cori away from her mother. She again thought about staying, but since she didn't entirely understand what was happening, she had to assume time might be a factor in solving it.

Every Cinderella story had midnight.

Every western had high noon.

Her situation was more like a venomous snakebite that required an antidote, but regardless of the metaphor, there were only three men that could help her out of this jam, and she had to get to them.

2

GYPSY GRACE HATED WAITING. It wasn't simply about being bored, but more about the space between one activity and the next. She hated the space. As far as she was concerned, every bit of her time should be productive. She was the queen of type A personalities and she was damn proud of it.

After three more seconds of inactivity, she ripped the walkie-talkie off her hip and made a choking sound into it. "Do you hear that?" she asked the persons on the other line. "That's my patience dying."

A laughing sound came over the line before Danato's voice cut in. "I'm working on it, Gypsy." He was using his low, calming voice that never actually worked on her, but he still insisted on trying.

"I'm going to throw myself off this fucking roof if you two don't get your asses in gear."

"Ethan's almost got her," Danato relayed over the device. "Are you ready?"

"Really?" she asked sarcastically, lifting her rifle onto her shoulder, even though he couldn't see her doing so.

"Forget I asked," he said. She could sense the smile behind the comment and she couldn't resist a smirk before she reattached the radio to her hip.

"Gypsy!" Ethan's voice came over. "She's coming fast!"

Gypsy didn't bother responding; she just repositioned her rifle to aim off the roof of the prison where she expected the creature to come up. She fired at the first sign of movement, but she missed. "Son of a bitch!" she yelled. She hated missing. It was a waste of ammo.

The reddish-brown bundle of feathers circled above her, then dive-bombed her. She waited for the creature to get close and she side-stepped the impending attack. A last-second thrust with the butt of her gun sent the creature scrambling to recover. The roughly one-hundred-pound half bird, half human skidded across the graveled roof, and massacred a fan vent.

"Seriously?" she droned. "Can't you crash in a way that doesn't hurt Danato's budget?"

"My apologies. I didn't see it there." The creature spoke with a breathy, feminine voice as she adjusted her wing feathers. If anyone in the real world had seen an Ekek, they would have assumed that they were seeing an angel. The body was human—give or take the abnormalities in the torso, which allowed for wing support. The females lacked breasts, and the males had internal genitalia. Their wings came in an array of colors, but primarily they were browns and grays.

The Ekek was no bigger than an anorexic ballerina, but Gypsy knew better than to underestimate her size. If that lesson hadn't been hammered into her head after two years of working with Belus the underdog, she was truly not paying attention.

"Gypsy, we have a problem," Ethan's voice sounded over the walkie-talkie.

"Kind of busy here," she mumbled as she took a shot at the creature. The dart hit firmly in the Ekek's leg, but she didn't flinch. Gypsy wasn't surprised. The medicine took at least thirty seconds to take hold.

"Don't shoot her!" Ethan's voice yelled over the radio.

Gypsy looked down at her hip, baffled by the words that had come over the radio. "What?"

"I found eggs in the duct. Empty eggs. Don't shoot her!"

The Ekek unhinged her jaw and opened her mouth wider than a human mouth would be capable.

"No." Gypsy shook her head. The creature's grating shriek was similar to that of a hawk, but significantly louder.

Gypsy walked away from the bird, cursing. She cracked her neck and rolled her shoulders as she distanced herself from the mother. She ripped the walkie-talkie from her hip. "You know, just once it would be nice if this shit would go to plan."

"I'm already on my way," Ethan said, huffing into the radio.

"Good luck with that. She's already called them. How many eggs?"

"You don't want to know."

"Ah... actually I do. How will I know when I'm done?"

"Eight," Ethan said.

"Son of a—"

"I told you, you didn't want to know."

"I'm switching to bullets," Gypsy said.

"The hell you are," Danato's voice chimed in again.

"Danato," she said, "I've only got nine shots left."

"That ought to be one more than you'll need," Danato said with another hint of his smile looming behind his voice.

Gypsy didn't respond, partially because she didn't want to give him the satisfaction of asking for help, but also because a cherub with hellfire-red wings was coming right at her. She dropped the radio and bashed the butt of her gun into the winged brat.

It was difficult at first to associate something that looked like a baby with a deadly creature, but it only took one look at their flesh-ripping shark teeth to make her redefine her parameters of cute. If that wasn't enough, the second one gnawing on her leg as if it were a fresh batch of fried chicken put things into further perspective.

She shot the second one. At such close range she was still risking killing the little bugger, but given the amount of her blood streaking its face, she didn't really care. It fell away, and she heard three muted cries from above.

The triple attack forced her to roll and shoot. She missed with the first shot, but the next two dropped two. The third cherub veered off before she could get a good aim.

She felt a breeze behind her and dove forward out of the reach of two more baby Ekeks. They didn't miss a beat and barreled after her, half flying, half crawling as she crab-walked away from them. Their tiny little chins were wet with salivation. "Sick little puppies." Gypsy scrambled to kick them away, but they clamped onto her proffered boots as an appetizer.

She took it as good fortune and pinned the two beneath her boots. She shot each of them and kept them pinned while the dart took effect. The last two attacked her from behind by flight. She shot at them, but she wasn't used to shooting upside down and missed both times.

She did a quick count of her bullets and shot the closest devil baby. She grabbed a dart from one of her now sleeping pinned birds and loaded it. She shot the eighth one just as it plunged down at her. The not-so-angelic baby landed on her stomach, continuing to writhe. It didn't completely pass out, but as soon as its breathing slowed and its tiny little vicious teeth disappeared, she risked touching it to move it off her. Even in the drugged state, the little bastard tried to bite at her fingers.

She got to her feet and dusted herself off just as Ethan made it to the roof. He pointed the rifle he held at the sky, scanning for more vicious cherubs, but when he saw her, he lowered it. "You didn't even leave me one?"

"Too slow." She limped over to him. He glanced at her leg, but he didn't offer her any assistance.

"I made it out of that duct and up here in less than three minutes. I'd like to see you do that."

"I don't have to. I'm the front line. I start where the action is."

"Well, you're not perfect." He nodded to her leg.

"What, that?" She pulled up her pleated skirt and looked at the blood coursing from the missing chunk in her leg. It really did look bad. "Just another scar for my collection." She smoothed her skirt back down.

Ethan mumbled something before heading back to the roof exit. Another shriek pierced the calm and Gypsy raised her gun at the mother Ekek as she mustered just enough strength for one last lunge at her. The grand defiance of a mother protecting her young deserved more than one dart. She cursed herself for not thinking of that.

Her rifle clicked unsatisfactorily, but Ethan released two more darts that put the creature down in its tracks. With both their guns extended, Ethan faced her, still panting from his sprint to the roof. He was waiting for her to say thank you or offer some acknowledgment that he had done a good job.

She looked down at the creature. "Two? I think one would have sufficed. Do you think Danato is made of money?"

He glared. "Really? What about your ninth dart? That's a little reckless of you."

"Yeah, but I used one twice, so I more than made up for that." He shook his head and walked away. She followed closely. "What's that smell?"

"Shut up."

"She must have been cooped up in that vent for a while."

"Shut up."

"Ekek shit." She hissed. "That's a tough smell to get out. I guess you'll be doing a buzz cut again." Ethan abruptly turned around and hugged her, smearing the scent on her. It was a bold move for him, but she imagined he only did it because he knew she was out of darts. "Oh, son of a bitch!"

He laughed. "What's wrong, Gyps?" She squirmed against his vice grip on her waist, pressing her palm into his chin. He was being very careful not to touch her anywhere above or below her midline. He knew better.

"Don't get that in my hair or I will kill you in your sleep."

He let her go and walked away. "What does it matter? You'll just bleach your hair and change the color again."

"Yeah, well, I like the purple," she said, shaking her purple pigtails for effect.

He glanced back and smiled. "Yeah, I like it too."

3

G YPSY FREELY UNDRESSED IN front of Ethan when they reached the incinerator receptacle. She slipped off her pleated skirt, double shirts, and her leggings. She probably could have kept them, but they were white and covered in blood, so why bother? Ethan didn't flinch at her bare-essential undergarments. Any questions there had been about attraction between them had long since been dismissed by her. He had better offers anyway.

Ethan slipped out of his unvarying black t-shirt and cargo pants, leaving him in his dark gray boxer briefs. He was an attractive young man. She had always admired how he had bloomed from a skinny little runt to the daunting muscular specimen he now was. If there were any chance that she could ever be with a man again, she would have wanted it to be Ethan, but for now, she was content being without a partner.

Gypsy collected her tactical belt and gun before leading the way to the infirmary. The nursing staff took one look at her and jumped to get her a gown. They directed her to an exam station just off the main nursing station. After a frantic collection of bandages, needles, and antiseptics, the mood changed from urgent action to maternal controlled panic.

Ethan came to lean against the entrance to the exam room, casually sporting his underwear like a trained model. More than one nurse at the main station took notice of him. As they should—there were few male specimens around to enjoy, and fewer of Ethan's appeal.

"Ladies, you're doing a fine job," he announced with a game show host's baritone. "I want the best of care for my friend. No expense spared." The nurses obliged him with mincing giggles.

Gypsy chuckled as well, but not because she thought Ethan was funny. He recognized her cavalier amusement and glared at her.

"Gypsy, sweetheart, I'm going to give you a local anesthetic in your leg." The oldest nurse spoke to her as if she was infirmed. She wasn't sure if it was her visible scars or rumored scars that caused every woman in the prison to treat her with kid gloves. Despite her obvious thick skin, she never seemed to convince any of them that she wasn't a fragile china doll.

"Why?" Gypsy asked from her supine position on the bed.

Ethan threw a hand full of tongue depressors at her from the cart he was leaning next to. "For the pain, twit."

Gypsy guffawed. "I can't feel anything. It's too deep."

"Well." The nurse glanced at Ethan as if he might have some influence over her. He shrugged, assuming no responsibility for her. "Okay, I'm going to clean the wound now." The woman began pouring alcohol into the wound, and Gypsy screeched in pain. "Oh, I'm sorry!" The nurse scrambled for the anesthetic.

"I'm kidding." Gypsy laughed. "I seriously can't feel anything."

The nurse gawked at Gypsy's ill-mannered humor and stabbed the needle into her leg, anyway. Gypsy wasn't able to contain the yelp from that assault. "Better safe than sorry, dear." The nurse smiled, but Gypsy got the feeling she might have finally succeeded in pissing her off once and for all.

The nurse continued to debride her wound with generous pressure. She could still feel some of it, but knew better than to ask for more anesthetic. When Gypsy caught Ethan's eye over her shoulder, they both had to stifle laughter.

“WHAT THE HELL ARE you two doing?” Danato asked as Gypsy and Ethan came into the office in a hospital gown and underwear, respectively.

“Reporting.” Gypsy looked to Ethan for confirmation of the obvious. Ethan matched her mock confusion. “What does it look like we’re doing?”

Danato opened his mouth to respond, but shook away whatever he’d intended to say. “What’s the report?”

“Mother’s alive, but down,” Gypsy proceeded as intended. “Eight babies down, two might not have survived. I got a hunk out of my thigh, but it’s scrubbed and stitched. Oh, and Ethan smells like shit.”

“Thank you,” Danato said as he glanced at Ethan, “but I didn’t exactly miss that.”

Ethan threw his hands up. “I’m waiting to be dismissed so I can shower.”

“Dismissed, please.” Danato waved him out.

Ethan left just as Belus walked in. Belus didn’t flinch at his partial nudity, but he scrunched his nose after the lingering odor hit him. “The guards have collected the Ekeks," he said, glancing at Gypsy. "What was your damage?"

"Leg." She whipped back her gown and peeled back the bandage for him to see.

"Nerve damage?" he asked.

"Definitely."

"Big scar?"

Gypsy gave him two thumbs up. Belus seemed to understand the pride that came with a good scar. He wasn't nearly as squeamish about her near-death encounters as everyone else.

"If you two masochists are finished, can I get my report, Belus?" Danato grumbled.

"Three of the babies are dead," Belus said, "but the mother is safely ensconced in her nest. What do you want me to do with the five remaining?"

Danato tapped his finger on the desk as he considered his options. "Execute them."

"Excuse me?" Gypsy asked, even as Belus turned to leave. She shoved the chair behind her with her foot. It slid into the door, effectively stopping Belus's exit. He returned to Danato's desk and stood on the side. He all but waved the flag for the ensuing argument.

"I'm not letting them live, Gypsy. We don't need that mother trying to get to them, and I don't need them forming a horde."

"Yeah, I get that. Fuck 'em, I don't care, but why didn't you just let me use my pistol instead of a dart gun? I could have knocked off every last one of them with one magazine and some to spare."

"Because that's not how it works."

Gypsy glanced at Belus. He nodded in agreement. "So *you* can exterminate them, but I can't?"

"That's exactly right," Danato said, stiffening his back. "Is that a problem?"

It was far more dangerous Danato's way, but Gypsy wasn't surprised he didn't want her haphazardly killing an inmate's offspring. There was a fine line between self-defense and preemptive offense in this place, and it was probably best that Danato be the one to draw it. She shrugged. "Nah, it was more fun this way." She turned on her heel and headed to the door. She shoved the chair back in place. "I have to go," she announced, to give Danato the opportunity to dismiss her with his lazy wave. "I have a head to shave," she said before she left.

C ORI HADN'T EXPECTED ANY less than three guards with rifles pointed at her head when she exited the semi-trailer. The prison was a high-security facility and took stowaways very seriously. When there was only one armed guard sent to deal with her unexpected arrival, she was a little insulted. Ungracefully, she disentangled her leg from a strip of bubble wrap and smiled at the familiar face.

"Hi, Duke," she said with relief at seeing anyone she knew from her pre-wish life.

Duke's brow knit tightly before he lifted his rifle for a proper aim. His eyes fluttered over her in examination, but his hands stayed rock steady, with his finger already on the trigger. "Who are you, and what are you doing here?"

"I'm an employee of Danato's, or at least I was. I have to speak to him directly. It's urgent."

"How…? He…" Duke clearly wasn't sure how to handle this. Trespassers were generally wiped by whatever psychic was on good behavior and sent back to their place of origin. Cori already knew too much to simply be whammied and sent on her way. "I need to make a call."

"Please do," Cori said, crossing her arms and looking around with the casual boredom of someone waiting for a bathroom stall. The dock manager glared at her through the fog of his cigarette at the far end of the dock. She was certain that there would never be a time or dimensional schism that he didn't hate her and every other human being on earth.

"Miss, what's your name?"

"Cori... Reiger, or Pierce—that was never really established."

Duke relayed the information into the walkie-talkie a few more times before the other end stopped asking him to repeat it. She wondered how hard it was going to be to convince Danato that she *was* in his employ, but that she rubbed a lamp and made everyone, except her, forget it. At least this was one catastrophe caused by honest absentmindedness and not intentional ambiguity. That should earn some points.

"Miss?" Duke said as if he might be interrupting her. "I need to take you to the office."

She smiled at him. He always sounded apologetic to her, as if he was sorry that he had to exert anything resembling authority over her. She imagined that his mother had been tremendously exacting in her rules regarding the treatment of women.

Duke was torn between letting her lead the way—as a "ladies first" gesture—and guiding her to the office. Since she already knew the way, but she didn't exactly want to have a gun at her back, she did her best to walk just one step ahead of him. "How have things been here?" she asked when the silence seemed to demand some kind of filler.

Duke nearly lost his balance going up the stairs to the office hallway, but he recovered and nodded at her. "It's been just fine, Miss, thank you for asking." After a brief pause, he added. "And with you, miss?"

She sighed. "I accidentally rubbed a lamp, and I completely erased my life here."

Duke stopped midway down the hall and looked at her. She turned to face him. "I'm sorry to hear that. Those wily genies have been a pain in my buttocks as well."

Cori smiled at his reference to buttocks over ass. No swearing in front of the ladies. "Thank you, Duke. I only hope I can convince everyone else as easily as you."

"I've never been much for fibbing, miss, so I just assume that nobody else is either. I've been wrong on a number of occasions, but that doesn't mean I'm going to change my ways. If that makes me a simpleton, then so be it, but I'd hate to miss out on something wonderful just cause I didn't believe it to be true."

"That's a fine way of looking at life, Duke. I respect that, and maybe someday I can learn to be the same. Might keep me out of trouble." She smiled and rolled her eyes.

He smiled warmly, albeit uncomfortably. After a moment, he cleared his throat. "I beg your pardon, miss, but I still have to take you to the office."

She nodded, stifling a giggle. "I know, Duke." She continued down the hallway as he instructed. She was going to have to hang out with Duke more often when she got back to her reality. He seemed to be the type of man she could turn to for an honest opinion on just about anything.

Duke knocked on the glass-windowed door before pushing it open and directing her inside. He stayed outside, no doubt to avoid removing his weapon. She expected to see Danato behind the desk, but it was Ethan. She smiled at him, happy that he was here and still him. His hair was shorter, and he didn't mirror her joyful relief, but it was him. He lifted himself out of Danato's chair and circled around to examine her.

"She's unarmed," Duke offered.

"Clearly," was all Ethan said in return. "Dismissed."

"Yes, sir." Duke reached for the knob.

"Thank you, Duke," Cori said, since Ethan wouldn't give him any kudos for his performance.

"You told her your name?" Ethan glowered at Duke.

"No, sir, she already knew it." Duke closed the door before any other questions or accusations could be posed.

Ethan approached and stalked around her, critiquing her as if she were a statue being submitted for an art show. "Who are you? How do you know about this place? Who sent you?"

"Ethan..." She started to explain, but he clamped onto her face and shoved her head back so he was effectively above her.

"Don't toy with me. Whatever your plan is, I will find out. You might as well tell me everything. Who are you?"

"I'm your wife."

6

TELLING SOMEONE YOU'RE MEETING, theoretically
for the first time, that you are their spouse is a bit
like saying that if you multiply six times nine, you get
forty-two. Sure, someone is bound to find it amusing, but
no one will believe you.

"Bullshit," Ethan said, releasing her face.

He didn't get the humor.

"Look..." Cori rubbed her cheeks where he had
pinched her. "I know that right now in this version of
reality, I'm not your wife, but in my version, I am."

Ethan laughed. It was late, but she was happy that he
wasn't getting angrier. "Why in the hell would I believe
this?" He propped his hands on his hips and looked her
over again.

"I know you. I know this place. I can prove it."

"Really?" He stepped back and leaned against the
desk. "Okay, prove it."

"You came to this place a little over two years ago.
Danato purchased you from slave traders. He's been
molding you into his successor for the last two years. You
used to be a scrawny little half-pint, but after a little dragon

juice, you beefed right up. I used to think you were shy, but in reality, you're more reserved." She stepped closer to him. "You're observant, patient, and protective."

She touched his hand that was braced against the desk. She hoped memories weren't the only thing that bonded them together. "You were a virgin when Danato brought you here." His eyes widened ever so slightly at the insight. "Unless you've taken a leave of absence or found someone else, you're probably still a virgin."

Ethan held her gaze for a second more before sputtering into uncontrolled laughter. She yanked her hand away and brought back the distance between them. He applauded her mockingly. "That was the biggest load of crap I've heard in my life. Don't get me wrong, you got the back story right, but come on..." He wiped away a tear from his effortful glee. "You might as well have just said I'm a lazy poof. Virgin, yeah, that's priceless. I'll have you know there are several ladies that enjoy my company on a regular basis."

Cori turned away from him. She didn't want to know about any of that. This was not going as she had planned. Somewhere in the back of her mind, she'd thought it would be easy. How hard was it to convince the man you love that you are who you say you are?

"So, what's your real story, Mrs. Pierce?"

Apparently a good deal harder, when the man you love isn't the man you love. It was time for brutal honesty. "I need you to take me to the prop room to find a lamp," she said sternly.

"And why would I do that?" he said, mimicking her earnestness.

"Because all of this is wrong; I've been written out of this version of events, and I don't plan on letting it stay that way."

"Oh, let me rephrase that question. Why would *I* help you with that?"

Cori ran her fingers through her hair. This was not working either.

"Please don't tell me that it's because we love each other, because my breakfast is so precariously balanced in my gullet as it is."

"We..." Cori didn't know how to respond to this satire of their love and devotion, especially coming from the other half of the devoted party. "You do love me."

"I'm still waiting for the proof that you know me, let alone proof of my affections toward you."

Exasperated by the slow progression and frustrated by his pompous contempt for their relationship, she marched over to him and kissed him.

7

CORI FELT ETHAN GRIP her shoulders to pull her off, but in the heat of the kiss, his hands relaxed, and his lips received her. She pushed her arms under his, clutching his back. She let her mouth explore his as only a familiar lover could.

The tentative connection melted, and he kissed her back readily. His arms wrapped around her, and for a brief moment she was home again. Her joyous reunion lasted only seconds, though. He lifted her with easy strength, and laid her back on the desk. He climbed on top of her, kissing her more hungrily.

He reached to unbutton her jeans, and she realized she was not convincing him of anything. As far as he was concerned, a strange woman was throwing herself at him, and he was taking advantage of it. With no regard to her, Danato's desk, or the situation they were in, he fully intended to have sex with her right then and there. The details of who she was would be sorted out after he'd had his fun.

She pushed him away, but he didn't exactly go far. "Get off me." He lifted off her just enough that she could wriggle free of him. She adjusted her shirt, re-buttoned her pants, and tried to hide the shaking in her hands.

"What's wrong?" he drawled behind her. She didn't hear him get off the desk, so she assumed he was still lying on his side, waiting to see if she would return. "Why so shy all of a sudden?"

"I made a mistake." She crossed her arms, as if that would take away the feeling of his body against hers. "I thought you were my husband, but you're not. You're just somebody he would have become without me."

"I'll take that as a compliment. Your hubby sounds like a wuss."

"He's not—" She spun around and lost her gumption to fight for her husband when he was lying casually on top of the desk like it was a chaise lounge. "Would you get off of there?" Rather than wait for him to respond, she sat down in a chair in front of the desk. She was ready to resume a business interaction, sans intercourse.

He rolled away from her off the desk. She noticed, but ignored, the slight adjustment he made before sitting down again. "So," he said as he put his feet up on the desk and tented his fingers, mimicking Danato's heavy pondering position. "Why don't you start from the beginning?" he suggested without parenthetical denial.

"A couple years back when Danato purchased you, he also purchased me. We worked, studied, and trained under him. You and I competed and tied for the wardenship."

"Ha!" Ethan let out one condescending guffaw to interrupt her. "Now I know you're lying."

"I *did*," she said with a shrill objection. "I passed the written test with flying colors. Why does that surprise everyone so much?"

Ethan quirked a smile. "I meant I know you're lying because Danato would never let a woman compete for his job."

"Things are different between Danato and me. I'm like a daughter to him. Plus, I was going through a really... never mind. The point is, I'm your second-in-command. I'm Belus's successor."

"Mmm," Ethan said without any particular sarcasm. "Your boss by day, your... boss by night." He winked, but despite his carnal inference, his face remained taciturn.

"I'm not even going to begin to react to that blatant attempt to enrage my feminine independence, but just for the record, *I'm* the boss at night."

"I bet," he mumbled, before moving on. "What about Gypsy? Where does she factor into all this?"

"Who's Gypsy?"

As if on cue, the aforementioned woman entered the office. "Gypsy," Ethan offered his hand to display her. "She's the woman who came back to the prison with Danato and me. Gypsy, this is our stowaway."

8

GYPSY GRACE WAS 5'10" with a bit of extra weight, but that was hardly the first thing you noticed about her, since her hair was bright purple. Cori got the impression, by the black roots and frayed ends of her pigtails, that she was very familiar with bleach. As if the purple hairdo wasn't enough to put her as the lead of a Japanese anime character, she had a cute little black skirt, army boots, and a low-cut blouse that should have shown her cleavage except that she wore an undershirt to prevent it.

She was probably in her early thirties, but the outfit and hair made her look sixteen. She had porcelain skin that reminded Cori of Garr, except for a short scar along half of her left cheek, just in front of her ear. It was mostly obscured by a free-falling tendril of hair. Cori surmised from its severity that Gypsy was likely brought to this prison under as questionable circumstances as she herself had been. The only makeup she wore was black, tarantula-leg thick mascara and high gloss pink lipstick that she most likely applied habitually to keep it looking so wet. Despite the drama in her fashion, she was attractive.

It was easy to make assumptions about her by her appearance, but the holster she had strapped to her leg was proof that she was indeed one of Danato's favored employees. Cori had lost her gun shortly after getting it and she didn't seem to be making any progress toward getting it back. Gypsy had clearly not endured the same challenges that she had, or if she had, she'd just handled them better.

Cori pushed away the jealousy that inevitably reared its head when she met a woman she thought she had to compete with. She offered her hand to Gypsy, who had positioned herself up on Danato's desk without the propriety of crossing her legs. The skirt was luckily long enough not to make it vulgar, but it was clear that she wasn't concerned with the suggestion of it. "I'm Cori."

Gypsy grabbed a magnifying glass from behind her and comically examined her with it. All that was missing was the bubble gum she should have been chomping on and blowing bubbles with. Cori wasn't sure that she was trying to be cocky or funny, but either way, it was pissing her off. Gypsy stopped her examination when she reached her face, which by this time was probably wearing the scowl Cori hadn't been able to hold back.

"She's a bit of a stiff back, isn't she?" Gypsy smiled and hopped off the desk. She tossed the magnifying glass back to Ethan, who caught it and placed it back on the desk without moving more than an arm. "Gypsy Grace." She shoved her hand out to shake. Cori had since put her hand down, and now took this opportunity to make Gypsy wait for her to return the gesture.

Cori might have guessed that Gypsy was American just from her manners, but her dialect was too indistinct to make any further assumptions about her specific origins.

When Cori finally shook her hand and introduced herself again, Gypsy laughed. Cori ripped her hand back, which only spurred her on more. She was seconds from punching the woman in the face, but the office door opened and Danato marched in. "Danato, thank God," Cori said, forgetting that he didn't know her either.

She stood and pushed through Gypsy to get to him, but he backed away from her. His face was riddled with shock, and she thought, even fear. It was such a rare emotion for him that it was hard to recognize. "Olivia?" He whispered the name, as if Cori might confirm what his eyes couldn't interpret on their own.

She was about to correct him, but he dropped his cane and rushed to her. His oversized hands were embracing her face and tangling in the hair behind her ears at the same time. He was looming over her with so much intensity in his eyes that she couldn't speak. She didn't know this look. She didn't understand the emotions that were coming off him.

When he pressed his lips to hers with loving but non-paternal intent, she grabbed his arms, prepared to push him away. He pulled away from her before the kiss became something that she would have to seek therapy for.

"How is this possible?" he said to her, but she didn't have an answer.

"Boy, you really get around," Ethan said from his perch. Cori glanced over, but Danato's hands didn't leave room for her to give him a proper glare.

"Danato—" Cori started, but the familiar cock of a pistol at the door left both of them searching for the source.

Just outside the office door, Belus stood with Gypsy's pistol pointed right at Cori. He looked pissed and panicked. "Danato, step away from her. That's not Olivia."

"She..." Danato looked her over again, letting the differences he had ignored come to light. Cori wondered how subtle those differences had to be for him to make the mistake in the first place.

"She's not your wife, just ask her!" Belus was so forceful she thought she might want to keep Danato near her in case he really did shoot her. Eye for an eye was an overrated theory of justice.

Danato looked down at her for the answer that Belus had already asked. She drew in her brow sympathetically and caressed his cheek. She hated to see him in such agony. "No, Danato." She shook her head. "I'm not your wife."

He was away from her so fast she struggled to keep her balance. Belus stayed in the hall, not willing to enter with the gun, but she raised her hands to him to show she didn't intend to fight. "Belus, please don't—"

"How the hell do you know my name?" Belus barked.

"Who are you?" Danato jumped right in behind him.

"She claims to be your daughter," Ethan offered, still casually leaning back in his chair like potential weapons fire wasn't reason enough to get up.

"What?" Danato hollered.

Cori raised her hands up further and glared at Ethan. "Shut up! You are not helping!"

"I wasn't trying to," he said sternly, with a return glare that reminded her that he had no loyalties to her. She tried not to let that sting, but it really did.

"Explain yourself," Danato said with the low, threatening voice that he reserved for prisoners and disobedient guards. She was very familiar with it, but that stung too. She glanced at Belus, but there was certainly no hope of sympathy there.

She wasn't even aware that she was crying until Gypsy groaned. "Oh great, she's a crier too."

That was it. Cori was done with the whole situation. She wasn't sure that Belus wouldn't shoot her, but she was certain that Gypsy was going to get her ass kicked before that could happen.

Cori's elbow shot back into her nose, giving a resounding crack of cartilage. Gypsy had been unprepared for the attack and instinctively reached for her missing gun. Cori punched her in the stomach and, while she was hunched over, doled out a second hit to her kidneys.

When she heard the squeak of Danato's chair, she rolled back-to-back over her to avoid Ethan's grasp.

She grabbed Gypsy's arm and yanked her backward to the floor. Ethan tried to grab her, but he didn't understand Cori's purpose and only succeeded in keeping Gypsy from defending herself by grabbing her free arm. Cori pressed her foot into Gypsy's shoulder and twisted her shoulder the wrong way in the socket.

Gypsy screamed in agony. Ethan reached to dislodge Cori, but she braced herself and gave him a curt, disruptive noise that announced her intention to cause Gypsy more pain if he did. That particular threat brought a look of pure hatred to his eyes. She wondered if he felt something for this woman. She didn't want to think about that.

Ethan held up a hand to Danato before he could barrel him over to get to the fight. Cori saw Belus at the door. His expression had changed from anger to curiosity. His gun was slowly lowering. He must have recognized his signature move. "Belus," she said softly, "I think today's a whiskey day, don't you?"

His head tipped a little more, and the gun lowered completely. "Who are you?" He said it so softly she wondered if she would have heard it if Danato and Ethan hadn't been keeping perfectly still.

Cori released Gypsy's arm slowly. Gypsy looked pissed, but she understood that the time to fight back was over.

"I'm Corinthia Ellen Reiger. I was formerly the runner-up to succeed Danato, but I rubbed a damn lamp."

9

H AD CORI KNOWN ANYTHING about Gypsy, her temper, or her ego, she never would have let her go. But since she didn't, she did, and Gypsy's belated defensive response was a kick to the head that sent her into the wall. As soon as she regained a margin of balance, Ethan slammed her against the wall with such force that she saw stars in her vision.

"You don't touch her again. You understand?" he ground out, spitting through his teeth.

Cori couldn't even respond to that. Too many questions arose from his act of chivalry for his partner. Instead, she just stared at the man she'd thought could never be violent toward her.

"Ethan." Danato didn't offer any further demand, but he let go and Cori tried her best not to let her sadness show. Ethan turned away and made a concerted effort to calm down before facing her again.

No one helped Gypsy up, but Danato did mouth, "You okay?" to her when she was back on her feet. Gypsy gave him a nod before offering Cori a look that told her this fight wasn't over. Cori mentally chastised herself for creating an enemy so early in her plan. Or perhaps it was enemies, since her husband didn't seem to like her very much either.

Belus and Danato exchanged looks. Neither of them could deny the possibility, even if it was an impossible possibility in their minds. Still, they needed to be convinced. She stepped away from Gypsy enough to offer her surrender and waited for the interrogation to begin.

Gypsy had already taken a position on the edge of the desk. Despite her scowl that promised vengeance, she seemed to be the only one at ease enough to get comfortable. Ethan stayed within reach of Cori with his jaw set and arms tensed. He was prepared to tackle her if she posed any further threat. Belus had given up his firearm to enter the office and couldn't seem to take his eyes off her. He was, for once, completely awestruck by the situation at hand. Danato was still standing. His face was a mash of converging emotions: not quite angry, not quite shocked. If she had to guess, she would have thought he looked crestfallen.

"What lamp?" Danato asked, breaking the silence and engaging the interrogation sans two-way mirror and stale coffee.

"I don't know which one exactly. It's the one in the prop room with the tattooed Mr. Clean guy living in it. He won't answer me when I call to him. I've tried to wish away my wish, but nothing has changed."

"That's not really how it works," Belus pointed out. "What *did* you wish for?"

"I wished for things to go back to normal," she admitted.

"And did they?" Danato asked.

Cori smiled, even though her eyes were watering again. "I went back to my old home with my mom and some guy who I'm apparently dating."

"That's normal for you?" Danato asked.

"No." She shrugged, losing her humorous façade. "I guess so, maybe once upon a time." She laughed a little and briskly wiped her eyes. "I guess one should be careful what they wish for." Cori looked at Ethan, but he didn't have any sympathy for her pain. She looked at the floor, but it wasn't offering any more counsel than the people in the room.

She could hear the clock tick over the silence. She remembered how much the clock had annoyed her before, but now it almost seemed reassuring. It felt like a heartbeat. She looked back at Danato, who had since exchanged another look with Belus. "I'm sorry for screwing things up again." Her tears were beyond control. She hated that Gypsy was right about her, but she didn't understand the stress she was under. "I'm sorry I forgot about the lamp, but I just want to come home. I don't know how to do that without your help." Cori looked between Danato and Belus. She wasn't sure who she needed right now. Belus was the level-headed one, but Danato had no emotional investment in her at the moment, so he might be the deciding factor in her fate. "I'll answer any questions you have. I'll take any test you want. Just don't turn me away."

"Corinthia, you have to understand," Belus interjected. "We have no idea who you are."

"Just Cori, and I know, but if you give me a chance, I can prove it."

"How?"

"I can tell you Danato's favorite food. I can tell you Ethan's life story before he was brought here. I can tell you who you're dating in the cafeteria... and the infirmary." Cori raised her brow at Belus, but the response she got was a cold glare. She wilted and turned back to the floor. It still wasn't making her feel better. She decided that coyness wouldn't make any leeway with these men, so she pulled her chin up. "I can tell you the three vulnerable spots on Penelope."

"Who's Penelope?" Ethan asked.

"The dragon you have stored in the gym."

"Is that what this is about? Are you here for the dragon's blood?" Danato seemed to rise an inch or two higher with this potential threat.

Cori cringed in disgust. "No, Danato. I'm..." She sighed and cussed under her breath. "Take me to Cleos."

"How do you know Cleos?" Danato asked.

"What part of this don't you guys get? Danato purchased me two years ago with Ethan; you've been like a father to us. Ethan, you... I already explained this to you. Belus, I am your successor. I also happen to be a pain in your ass, but you can't help but like me." Cori raised her hands, waiting for enlightenment to strike them like lightning.

"What about me?" Gypsy asked humbly from the corner of the room. Cori looked at her. "What are we to each other?" There wasn't any sarcasm or suspicion in her voice; she was just curious.

Cori shook her head. "Nothing. In my version, you aren't here." Gypsy was offered several looks that might have been concern, but everyone hid it well. Ethan gave her a longer look before turning a glare back at Cori. Apparently, everyone was disappointed to hear that Gypsy was not always a part of their lives.

"Danato," Cori whispered. "Just take me to Cleos to prove my story, and then let's find the lamp and find out how to use my next two wishes to undo this." There was another fleeting set of looks to Gypsy before Danato agreed to take her downstairs. Belus offered to join, but Danato asked him not to. As Cori left the office, she could see Ethan was happy to stay behind to speak with Gypsy.

It's called heartache for a reason.

10

C ORI COULD FEEL THE tension in the elevator as she and Danato rode it down to the basement. It reminded her of the time he took her to see Vince. She glanced up at him, but he kept his head straight forward, grimly watching the semi-circle dial above the door slowly descending to the left. Considering it was only one floor, it took forever.

"Is there something you want to say?" Cori asked, noticing that his lips were parting in preparation for speech.

He slammed his thumb into the stop button—as if the ride wasn't long enough. "I need to apologize for how I behaved earlier."

"You mean kissing me?"

Danato clasped his hands in front of him. "Yes. I was confused."

"You thought I was your—"

"Very confused," Danato interjected.

"Why exactly would you think that?" she asked, daring to tread into his privacy.

"I was confused," he ground out.

Cori nodded. He had already made it clear to her that he would never discuss his wife with her. This Danato was not any different. "Good to know things haven't changed that much. You be sure and let me know if you change your mind about sharing your life with me." Cori yanked out the stop button. "Lord knows *I've only* sacrificed my freedom and future to serve you." He must have registered the irritation, but since he wasn't the one who had been sequestering his life from her, he didn't have any response or rationalization to offer more to her. Not that her Danato would have either, but at least he would have had the common decency to be hurt by her words.

She crossed her arms and spent the remainder of the ride pouting about something she didn't even know she had been that bothered by. At least she could depend on Cleos to be her ally in this mess.

11

"WHAT DO YOU MEAN?" Cori gripped Cleos's hand through his barred cage. Without her to plead for his soundproof cell, he was still behind bars, literally.

"I can't read you," Cleos grumbled. His hair, as usual, looked kempt aside from begging to be placed in a petite ponytail at the base of his neck. He wasn't a vampire, but all of his features—hollow cheeks, lanky body, and sun-deprived skin—screamed "stake me through the heart."

Cleos detested the vampiric photophobes he neighbored and took offense to any reference to similarities between them. He was an intellectual at heart, though he didn't have a specific subject of interest. His favorite thing had always been catching up on Cori's latest gossip by reading her mind. Cori had agreed to the reads until she'd realized that he was eating her memories.

The last time they had encountered each other, she had accidentally taken enough of his power, via her enchanted rings, to enter *his* mind, instead of the other way around. His subconscious had tried to stop her, but she got through to see his deepest, darkest secrets. There is really no way to apologize for breaking into someone's mind.

Cleos had been angry about the violation, but he was even angrier that she forgave him for his crimes after seeing what had prompted him to commit them. Cori also wasn't sure how one was supposed to apologize for offering clemency, but she hoped that Cleos would just get over it.

"No, that's just the rings," Cori explained. "Try to…" She gripped his hand tighter, and he examined the contact as if he wasn't used to someone being this close or comfortable with him, which in this version of things was probably true. "Cleos, you *have* to read me. You've never not read me." The tingling sensation that precluded her absorption of his power was gone as well. She couldn't read him either. "This isn't right," she said, mostly to herself.

"Do you know this woman?" Danato asked Cleos.

Cleos looked to him like he was stupid for asking. "Am I familiar with the woman you just brought down to see me? No."

Cori banged on Cleos's bars, and he drew back like she was the one behind the bars. "This isn't right. Why can't you read me?" Cleos had always been Cori's go-to backup. When things got too far out of hand, it was usually his help that brought things into perspective. He had even helped save her marriage, which was rather ironic since he had been the reason it nearly broke up. He was always there when she needed him and he had no idea who she was, and worse yet, he couldn't read her to find out.

"I generally have a few people I can't read," Cleos said. "Some are naturally immune. Others are blocked by overriding magic."

Cori looked at Danato. The explanation dawned on several levels. "The genie—he must be overriding Cleos, and my rings."

"What do your rings have to do with anything?"

"They're enchanted, but never mind that." She waved her hand. "We need to get to that lamp. I have to see the genie."

Danato grimaced. She knew that look. It meant that he really wanted to be obliging, but the rules said otherwise. She couldn't imagine there was a protocol for "woman shows up claiming to be the victim of a genie displacement," but she was pretty sure if there was, it would advise in bold print to "be as suspicious as hell."

"What?" she drawled.

"I can't take you to the lamp. The power they possess is magnificent. In the wrong hands, it could—"

"Could cause me to be displaced from my home, my friends, and my family? Yeah, got that memo a little late," she said. Danato didn't express any humor at her sarcasm, nor did he seem to have any interest in bending the rules for her. "Okay, obviously you don't know me, so bending the rules is not an option." Cori patted her hands together. "What do we need to do?"

"What do you mean?"

"I'm sure protocol dictates that you lock me up until my true purpose is revealed, but I'm begging you not to do that. There must be a way to find out about me. A test, a lie detector, or maybe we can just go see..." Cori nearly gagged trying to say Mezula's name. She didn't want to have anything to do with her, even if that meant taking a longer road to getting proof of who she was. "Anything."

Danato looked her over. She was apparently asking a lot not to be locked up. "I'll need to speak to Belus. He might have some ideas about what to do. In the meantime, I will need to have you guarded."

Cori nodded. "I understand." She was more than agreeable to that prospect. She was looking forward to talking with Ethan again. He was still going to be her best chance at getting this figured out.

12

C ORI HADN'T PLANNED ON Danato choosing Gypsy to guard her, especially since she had just kicked her ass. On the other hand, he probably figured it would give Gypsy a chance to redeem herself and earn back her pride.

With her pistol firmly in hand, Gypsy showed the same detached authority that all the guards showed. Even though she had to be feeling sheepish at her comeuppance at the hand of a veritable stranger, she hid it well.

While Belus and Danato argued in the office about how to handle the new troublesome female in their life—an argument that unified timelines and realities—Gypsy walked Cori down to the gym. Cori was relieved to see Ethan in the gym, waiting for them. "Ethan—" she started to say, but he tossed her a sword from a display near the entrance, interrupting her thoughts. "What is this?" She looked at the weapon.

"A rematch." He tossed Gypsy one as well. She caught it and holstered her gun. Ethan, in turn, un-holstered his and took the job of guarding her while Gypsy did some warmup swings with her sword.

"Great," Cori mumbled, leaning on her sword. "I don't suppose I can just apologize for kicking your ass and be done with it?" Cori glanced back at her, but she didn't answer. She wasn't listening anymore. Her mind was focused on her meditative warmup.

"Not likely," Ethan offered for his partner as he leaned against the wall by the door. "It was a cheap shot, anyway. She deserves retaliation for that alone."

Cori wanted to object, but he was probably right. She'd had the upper hand with her surprise attack. "I'm not very good with the sword. Belus has mostly been training me in hand-to-hand combat. I only use the sword when I fight the dragon."

Ethan repositioned his gun momentarily to offer her double mock violins with his fingertips. "Excuses, excuses."

She couldn't get over how arrogant he was. He reminded her of an immature high schoolboy who didn't open his mouth unless it was to insult someone or to make a crude joke. She didn't like this Ethan.

"Ready," Gypsy announced behind her. Cori looked back and saw her in perfect form, with her sword directly up and down. That must have been the appropriate starting position for a sword fight.

Cori cussed and lined up in front of her. "This is just mock sword play, right? I mean, we aren't playing for fingers or anything, are we?" No one offered an answer.

As soon as Cori's starting position was locked, Gypsy attacked. The clang of the sword was not so much the melodious ting of a television sword fight, but the clank of metal on metal. It probably sounded better from a distance, but to Cori it just sounded like trash can lids being slammed onto their bases.

She should have been prepared for the vibration, but there was a big difference between hitting dragon scales and hitting another sword. She was certain that, if she hadn't been afraid for her life, she would have scratched the painful tickle from her palms.

Gypsy was good. Clearly, this was where she was proficient. The sword may as well have been an extension of her arm. She batted away all of Cori's sluggish attacks and forced her back with each impact of the sword.

To add madness to misery, Gypsy started doing backflips and handless cartwheels to avoid Cori's last-ditch lunging attacks. It was bad enough that she was better at swordfighting than Cori, but to practically be a gymnast was just the type of slap in the face Cori didn't need right now.

Cori wanted to just give up, but that wasn't the point of this. She needed to bend over and take her spanks like a good little girl. She danced around, doing her best to avoid the hits, but Gypsy aptly cultivated her revenge with five or six gentle jabs and broadside pats to her torso. By the time the so-called rematch was done, Cori's ego was on the floor wallowing in dejected self-pity, while Gypsy was swaggering with the hip sway of a winner.

Gypsy tipped her brow to Cori, before meeting Ethan for a high five and elbow bump. He congratulated her on a triumphant win, and she offered a humble declaration that basically pointed out that Cori was pathetic. Therefore, the battle didn't deserve of any grandiose compliments.

Cori applauded her as she panted for her recovery. She offered it partially because Gypsy had earned it, but also because she wanted to break up the back-patting party. They both looked at her crossly, interpreting it as sarcasm, so she stopped. "That was amazing." They glanced at each other, not offering any comment until they knew her meaning. "No, really, I'm sure I'm not the best opponent for you, but I can see you are an excellent swordsman."

"You think I need you to tell me that?" she said, wagging her head and bringing her sword to rest on her shoulder.

"No, I imagine you don't, but I think the compliment is in hearing *me* say it."

Gypsy smiled. "That it is, but I would have been just as satisfied with you curling into a fetal position and bawling."

Cori bit her lip so she didn't retort with a scathing curse that would no doubt incite a bigger argument. She was good at humility since her self-esteem never let her get too pompous, but she was not good at sycophancy. "I imagine, at first glance, someone as strong-minded as you might think that about me. Needless to say, you can think what you want about me, but it's been a really long couple of days for me, so you'll have to forgive me if I don't rise up to your high standards of feminism."

Gypsy scoffed at her comment, but Ethan seemed less amused by the statement. He eyed Cori carefully, seeing something different in her. "Now my turn," he announced, and approached her.

"You've got to be kidding. Haven't I already proved my ineptness with a sword?"

"Yes, you have." He took the sword from her hand and tossed it to Gypsy. She caught it gracefully and took both of them back to the rack on the wall. "Let's try your skills at hand-to-hand combat."

"Oh, please!" Cori said.

"You think you're that good?" Ethan asked, misinterpreting the direction of her cynicism.

"No, I think I don't fight men who can bench press four times their body weight."

He glanced back at Gypsy, who crossed her arms in response to Cori's intimate knowledge. "I'll go easy on you. Don't we mock fight in your version of reality?" he asked, advancing slowly, making the space uncomfortable.

"Danato would never allow that," she said, trying to turn her body, so her retreat appeared to be a change in direction, rather than the back-pedaling it really was.

"He doesn't allow me... the other me, to fight my own wife? Doesn't he trust me?"

"I don't know if he forbids it for my safety or his ease of mind… or your discomfort." Ethan quirked an eyebrow, not understanding her meaning. "It's a long story, but let's just say you would be very distraught at inflicting any lasting pain on me." He paused his advance.

"He," he pronounced the word carefully, but it didn't lend any reason for it being spoken.

"Excuse me?" she asked.

"*He* would be distraught at hurting you, not me," Ethan clarified.

Cori looked him up and down. He looked like her Ethan, but he was very much not him. Two years and a thousand different variables had changed his motives and devotions. "Clearly," she said, hoping that it might hurt him a little, but knowing it wouldn't.

"Your Danato isn't here. My Danato isn't here. What do you say to a little one-on-one?" An index finger curl begged Cori to attack, but she didn't. She looked at Gypsy, hoping that she might have the rational mind to break this up. She, however, had settled into the wall just as Ethan had earlier. All she needed was a cigarette and a fist full of twenties and she would have been placing bets on this cock and hen fight. "Come on, Mrs. Pierce."

She sighed and rolled her shoulders back. She never would have been nervous fighting her Ethan, despite Danato's concerns. He had always been careful with his strength. This Ethan, however, was egotistical, brazen, and lewd. She had no doubt in her mind that this was just his excuse to get his hands on her again. She wasn't sure it was possible to be afraid of the same face that she loved, but the possibility was rapidly turning to probability.

"What the hell!" Cori said abruptly and clapped her hands. "Gypsy, it was nice meeting you. Ethan... not so much."

Ethan chuckled as he squared off into a wrestling stance. Cori did the same. They waited several seconds before either of them would move. Ethan must have gotten tired of waiting, which was another sure sign that this was not her husband. He lunged at her, and she spun out of his way, taking a kidney shot on the way.

He whipped around, barely affected by the move. He shoved her back, almost making her fall, but she regained enough purchase to kick him in the face when he charged again. She retreated, watching him check his face for blood. His head would never be affected by any number of her kicks or punches, but it didn't mean it wouldn't hurt.

She tried not to squeal when he cut off her retreat and lassoed an arm around her neck. She tucked her legs and let her body weight draw her through the crook of his arm. Once her butt hit the ground, she took a less than sportsmanlike crotch shot with her fist. Dragon juice or no, that particular region was still vulnerable.

Ethan groaned and hissed. She rolled away and shot up jackrabbit-fast. He glared at her, offended she had broken the cardinal rule of fair fighting. "I'm sorry, did we agree on no below-the-waist hits?"

"No, we didn't," he ground out.

She couldn't help but let a smile slip, which prompted another round of battle that was more kickboxing than wrestling. Cori was no longer thinking about a clever repartee. Belus's guidance and the memory of Efrat's many murder attempts focused her into survival mode.

Ethan must have noticed the change, because he increased his speed to meet her vigorous defensive tactics. She was impressed that he wasn't using his full strength. At least he wasn't a *complete* ass.

Cori managed to get in a punch to his stomach and an elbow to his face. He grabbed her from behind when the elbow receded, but she was already prepared for that.

Ethan's compacted muscle was certainly heavier than Efrat's, but under the strength of her legs, she still managed to flip him over her back. One gravitational body slam later and Cori drove her fist as hard as she could into the intercostal muscles of his ribs. He clenched his teeth in irritated pain.

Gypsy hooted by the door. "You go, girl!" She applauded.

Cori couldn't afford a glance at her, but Ethan did, and she tried to twist his shoulder out of socket like she had with Gypsy's earlier. Embittered by either Cori's slight upper hand or Gypsy's cheering duplicity, he growled and pulled back on his arm with full strength.

No match for his full strength, she was pulled over him and onto the floor. She would have preferred to skid across the glossy white floor, but Ethan kept hold of her hand, and she yanked to a stop as soon as she landed. With a quick tug on her arm, she was under him, with his hips pinning hers and his hands pressing her right hand and left shoulder down hard.

His panting mimicked hers, but not to the same degree. He was mad, to say the least. It wasn't every day that a few cheap shots got past him. She didn't bother fighting him. It had certainly always been his intention to win. It was just a matter of how long he let her flounder. His intention had probably been to watch her embarrass herself, or at least evaluate her skill. He was obviously displeased that she wasn't a complete klutz.

As his breathing slowed, he let his eyes travel her body. She wasn't sure how to feel about that. He looked up at Gypsy, who was offering a thumbs-up at the door. "Go find out what's keeping Danato and Belus. Either we're testing her or we're not." Gypsy gave a compliant nod and headed out the door.

"Gypsy," Cori called much too late, when she realized this was just his excuse to get her alone.

Ethan released her arm and shoulder, but stayed on top of her. "You're pretty good," he admitted.

"Belus is a good teacher," she said, looking at the door.

"Yes, he is. I recognize some of his work." He leaned on his hands to release some of the pressure on her hips. He was still straddling her, but now on all fours.

"Does that mean you're starting to believe me?"

He shrugged as best he could in his current position. "Anything's possible in this place, right?"

She nodded. "Yeah, it really is."

Ethan relaxed down slowly, putting the weight of his body back on her more evenly. He kept himself propped on his elbows so he could look at her. "I am starting to see how you and I could be an item." Cori didn't answer or even move. Too many different thoughts and too many different emotions were crowding into her mind to offer anything more than a blubbering sputter. He leaned down and kissed her lips, gently. It was familiar and unfamiliar, which unfortunately made it exciting. "What do you say we continue what we started in the office?"

She felt him shift against her and he moved in for another kiss. At the last second, she pulled her face away. "No."

"No?" He smiled. "Why not? I'm your husband, aren't I?" he whispered and kissed her neck.

"No, you aren't," she said, pushing him off and rolling away before he could pull her back. "My husband is kind, patient, and foolishly in love with me." She stood up and dusted herself off, even though the floor was always impossibly clean. He did the same. "You're just curious. Maybe I'm a good lay since I already know every inch of your body." He tipped his brow at that, but she ignored it. "You are Ethan Xavier Pierce, but you are not my husband. It might be easier just to forget that, but I have every intention of going back to him. I'm not entirely sure this constitutes cheating, but I'll be damned if I'm going to sleep with a man who doesn't love me."

"Huh, that is interesting," Ethan said.

The door to the gym opened and Danato, Belus, and Gypsy filed in. Cori added more distance between her and Ethan. Despite nothing really being interrupted, her face burned with embarrassment. Danato eyed the situation and gave Ethan a stern look of disappointment. Ethan only offered him a shrug.

"Well." Cori looked at Belus. He was still being cautious of her by keeping a good distance from her. She wasn't used to seeing Belus unsure of himself. It worried her. "What's the verdict?" When Belus didn't offer an answer, she turned to Danato.

"We will need to run some tests. You will need to remain confined."

Cori cursed under her breath and walked a few steps away. She bolted back to them, clenching her teeth and fists. "Just take me to the damn..." She stopped herself and pulled back again. Getting angry wouldn't make them trust her more.

Then again, what would?

"No, actually..." she reversed once again, taking back her temporary aphasia to face her would-be opponents and shake her finger in their faces. "I'm not going to let you three bulldoze my objective. I have offered you plenty of proof, starting with my direct knowledge of the existence of this place, let alone knowing details of your lives, but if you want to get more intimate..." Cori glanced back at Ethan, who was no more entertained by this display than any other she had put on.

"...Danato, you live in a living house, with hunter lodge décor that I detest, but that I can't help but call home. You get your newspapers in bulk each month, but they might as well be bedtime stories, because every other night you fall asleep with one in your lap. Your chili is way too sweet, but Ethan loves it, so I hold my tongue. You are fastidious and clean to the point of OCD, but I've learned to comply. You use too much salt, and by the looks of your belly, no one has been making heart healthy meals for you." Danato touched his stomach, which had a little more stuffing than a teddy bear of his size ought to have.

"You brought me here over two years ago and I fought you every day for months. Your thunderclap scoldings still make my knees shake, but I don't know anyone who has cared for me or protected me as earnestly as you have, including my birth father." Cori paused to let him feel that comparison before moving on to Belus.

"Belus, I wish I knew more about you, but the truth is, every ounce of personality that you've revealed to me has either been accidental or unwillingly extracted from your stubborn antisocial grip. All I can tell you is that I've disappointed you more than once, and I probably will again. If you continue to forgive me, it will only be because I am one of the few people in this world who has the ability to melt that ice cold device you call a heart. It takes a crowbar to get you to admit it, but you like me. You don't let me show you any affection though, because...well, you hate it, but also because you don't want to make Danato jealous of the bond we have." As expected, Belus didn't offer her much of an emotional reaction, but he furrowed his brow in consternation over the new information.

Cori turned to Ethan, who raised his brow and crossed his arms in preparation for his personality-revealing attack. "Don't act like you're immune to me. I know more about you than any of them. I've seen you naked inside and out. I know your wealthy parents died when you were young, taking you from a privileged life to an impoverished one." As she approached him, he seemed to lose his bravado. "I know you spent the remainder of your childhood in and out of foster homes. Your stint as an amateur thief put you in the juvenile system. You've been analyzed by enough psychiatrists that you have the language memorized. You occasionally turn it against me in my more irrational states.

"Coming here was the highlight of your life. I'm not even sure if Danato realizes how important it is for you to be part of a stable family, even if it is a little unorthodox. I think that's why we got married so fast. As caveman-ish as it sounds, I think you wanted to have that symbol of possession. You might downplay your territorial side, but I think when push came to shove, you would kill any man who tried to take me away from you."

Ethan's self-portrait must have scared him a little, because he took a step back and looked away from her. She was about to make another comment, but Gypsy jumped into the conversation.

"So, in your world, are you screwing all three or just Ethan?"

Cori's eyes widened as she turned to her. She couldn't believe she had taken everything she had just said and boiled it down to a bad soap opera plot. She flared her teeth for her planned retort. She lifted her hand to offer the finger jab of someone wanting to accurately direct their insult.

She barely got the seething, "You," out before a burst of flame spread from her directed finger. Gypsy shot back, trying to avoid the heat, but she nearly lost her eyebrows before she cleared the path. "Oh, shit," Cori mumbled before Ethan toppled her.

13

I T WASN'T A RECORD for Gypsy to be in the infirmary twice in one day, but Cori was getting a good number of lucky strikes against her, and that *was* unusual. Gypsy had to give the woman props for hand-to-hand combat. Belus—assuming Belus was the one who had taught her—must have been very dedicated to her training. She was useless with a sword, but most women were, since it requires a good deal of upper body strength. On the other hand, the fire-breathing fingers were something else altogether.

After the doctor evaluated the minor burns on her face and arms, Gypsy joined the three musketeers at the holding cell at the center of the infirmary. It was similar to a psychiatric holding cell with its plastic padded walls and windows just big enough to see through but not crawl through. The stark white interior did nothing to change the comparison, but since it was large enough to hold creatures weighing upwards of two tons, it made Cori's confines look like a chair-less waiting room.

When Gypsy arrived, Danato and Belus were still debating their next step while Ethan leaned against the wall, waiting for the decision. He normally didn't take such a back seat to these sorts of discussions, but she suspected Cori had gotten under his skin. He was probably already starting to believe her.

"How did she get the power?" Belus asked.

"She mentioned something about enchanted rings," Danato said. "She didn't elaborate. She was very upset that Cleos couldn't read her because of them."

"Or he couldn't read her because she doesn't want him to," Gypsy contributed as she approached.

Danato looked her over. She no doubt looked as if she had spent an hour too long in the sun, but otherwise, she was fine. "You think she's a reader?"

"Occam's razor, it's the easiest explanation for what she knows," she said, locking her thumbs into the waistband of her skirt.

"Maybe," Belus said, but it was only a diplomatic *I disagree.* "She didn't just offer facts, though. She didn't just mention that Danato likes chili, which she could easily read from him, but she also said she didn't like his chili because it was too sweet. That wasn't just a truth; that was an opinion. I doubt any reader would delve so deep as to discover taste, let alone bother to form an opinion on that taste."

"Even if she is telling the truth," Danato said, "do we really want someone with the ability to shoot fire running around the prison? Whatever power she has, it's strong, and I'm not sure we want to risk her forcing her way into the prop room."

"Why don't you just talk to the genie yourselves?" Ethan said, finally offering some useful thoughts.

Danato furrowed his brow and turned the question to Belus. "We can't initiate any contact or conversation with the genie without her being present or we risk becoming blessed with wishes ourselves. We can act on her behalf, but genies are logistical nightmares, and if she is lying..." Belus trailed off.

Danato knew right where to pick up. "Genies are essentially indentured gods. It's not entirely impossible to accidentally sign your life away when dealing with them. They are litigious, shrewd, and, unfortunately, tremendously powerful."

"You want to keep her locked up, then?" Gypsy asked.

"No, not really," Danato said reluctantly.

"Did I miss something?" Gypsy asked, seeing the visible stress in his eyes.

"In theory," Danato continued, "if she has been displaced by a genie, she has a limited amount of time to recant her wishes. If she doesn't do it before the window expires, she will be stuck here."

Gypsy chuckled at the volleying argument. She looked at Ethan, who was still remaining unusually quiet. "What about you, Buzz Cut? Care to weigh in on this balancing act? Is she one of us, one of them, or just batshit crazy?"

Ethan seemed annoyed at being forced into the debate, but after a moment he stood at attention and reported his thoughts military style: short, sweet, and with just enough attitude to sound convincing. "We need to proceed with medical testing to identify her. Then we need a slew of questions answered about those rings. If we can be satisfied that she isn't a threat, then and only then will we confront the genie."

Danato nodded. It wasn't often that he deferred to Ethan's preferences, but when he honestly didn't know which way to go, he welcomed Ethan's tactical summation of the situation.

"Well, let's get this girl poked and prodded alien abductee style." Gypsy started toward the door of the cell.

"Gypsy." Danato placed his hand in front of her, being careful not to touch her. "I don't think you are the best candidate to handle her. You've incited her twice already."

"Yes, and two of you have already kissed her today. Do you think *you* are the best candidate?" Danato's sympathy darkened into irritation. She had pissed him off, but she couldn't keep her eyebrow from ticking up to challenge him. His jaw clenched, and he sucked in a long breath, as if he were mentally counting before answering her challenge.

"I'll take her," Belus mumbled beneath them as if he were offering to throw down his life for a cause he didn't much prefer to be fighting for, let alone dying for.

Danato didn't take his eyes off Gypsy. His anger was useless on her, but he couldn't help but feel it. She had spent too much time in the hands of a violent man to be intimidated by his venomous looks or loud voice. Though Danato had never hit her, she had pushed him to the point of shaking her violently. Testing the gentlemanly resolve of her men was one of her favorite hobbies.

"I think that's best," Ethan said, bumping into her as he moved between her and Danato. The intentional push shoved her out of the line of Danato's glare. "We'll just get back to work until you need us again."

"That's an excellent idea," Danato said as Ethan continued to herd Gypsy away.

14

C ORI HAD MORE THAN a few regrets in life. She wished she hadn't released the elementals without speaking to Danato and Belus. She wished she hadn't killed that merman. She wished she hadn't pissed off Cleos by reading his mind. The list went on and on, but at the top of the list, she wished she hadn't wished for things to go back to normal.

Cori looked around the white padded cell in the infirmary that was designed for the observation of new prisoners. This was so far from normal, it wasn't even funny. Or perhaps it was so far from normal that it was hilarious. Either way, Cori wasn't in the mood for laughing. She just banged her head against the soft mattress-y walls and waited for someone to fetch her.

By the time Belus showed up at the window in the door, she looked certifiable. She made a droning sound as she buried her head in and out of the foam. It was a hypnotic rhythm that, for the moment, was comforting. Not to mention she was bored out of her mind.

"Cori?" Belus's voice sounded over the intercom, interrupting her not-so-Zen meditation.

She exhaled and moved over to the panel. There was no button to push, so it was either on or off, she presumed. "How is she?"

He nodded with a frown. "Okay. A little singed. She's probably more upset about her hair than the burns."

"I would be too. I suppose she'll be getting revenge for me hurting her pride."

"Gypsy isn't a proud person. She's just a perfectionist. She doesn't care if you win, as long as you win because you're good, and not because she wasn't at her best."

Cori gave him a half smile. "She's your star pupil, I guess."

"We need to do some tests on you," Belus said, changing the subject. She wasn't sure whether he had done it for her benefit or his, but she was glad to stop talking about her replacement. "Standard medical stuff. Can I assume you will cooperate?"

"If I can assume that you're working toward proving me right."

"You can assume that we're working toward finding the truth."

Cori smiled at Belus. "It's nice to know that you're consistent, no matter how inconsistent my life is."

Belus put in the code to unlock the door and opened it wide for her to leave. She stepped into the hall slowly and waited for him to shut the door. He pointed down the hall, and she took the lead, with him following behind her.

She glanced back, but each time she did, more distance had gathered between them.

"Step into the lab on your next right."

Cori turned into a room with an exam table and counters filled with equipment, the names of which she probably couldn't pronounce, let alone know what they did. "Is this going to hurt?" she said, hopping up on the table.

"No." He waved to a nurse before coming in. "Well, it does involve needles, so yes, but if you are who you say you are, you should be able to handle it."

"I don't know. I'm not your bravest employee." Cori chuckled, but let the levity die away when she realized there was no hope of making this a social situation.

"Okay, sweetheart." A round, jolly nurse with short salt and pepper hair came in with a toolkit of needles and test tubes. Cori didn't recognize her, but the nursing staff changed so often, it was hard to remember any of them. "We need to get some blood from you."

Though she sounded sweet, she strong-armed Cori to lie back on the table rather than ask. Cori tried to position herself to help the woman, but in the end she just went limp so the woman could situate her as she wished.

Belus remained stoic, watching her intently, waiting for her to defend herself or attempt an escape. "You really don't trust me at all, do you?"

"It's my job to be suspicious."

"Yeah, I get that, and obviously a complete stranger with magic rings claiming to know you would be pretty high on the suspect list, but... ouch." Cori winced at the bigger-than-normal needle being inserted into her arm. From the looks of the number of tubes the nurse had, she intended to do a lot of tests. "Do I get a cookie and juice after this?" The nurse ignored her quip.

"But what?" Belus asked, drawing her attention back to him.

"But you were aiming a gun at my face before you knew any of that. I've only seen you aim a gun twice. Both times at the same man, oddly enough. Once defending the prison, and the second time defending me. It takes a lot for you to pick one up. What set you off? Why were you so threatened by me?"

Belus stared at her with seemingly no intention of answering. She rolled her eyes and looked at the ceiling while the nurse finished her phlebotomy. After she finished labeling her tubes, she told Belus when to expect the results and left them alone. Cori kept her arm bent over her gauze bandage and waited for further instruction.

"You look like her," Belus said after a moment. Cori turned to him with her brow furrowed in the most obvious, silent question. "Olivia."

"That was Danato's wife. The one who died."

Belus's eyes closed gently, and they stayed closed until he spoke again. "I am suspicious of a familiar face making claims to get her near a very powerful tool."

"That's why he bought me, isn't it?" Cori asked rhetorically. "He only needed Ethan, but I reminded him of her. He couldn't resist."

"I don't know about any of that, but from my perspective, you are dangerous to Danato."

"You think I'm... what... taking this form to get close to him?"

"Something like that. All I know for sure is that I'm not letting him make the same mistake twice."

"What mistake?" Cori sat up. Belus shifted in response. "What happened to her? Why is he so damn secretive?"

"It's not my story to tell."

"Heard that before." Cori slipped off the table. Belus took a step back. "Stop cowering! Everything I know about combat, I learned from you, so I don't have a chance."

Belus's eyes narrowed. "I wasn't cowering. I was drawing back."

"Are we done?" Cori shifted to display her bandaged arm.

"For now." Belus said nothing more as the nurses performed the remainder of the tests, and neither did Cori. When it was all said and done, he returned her to her cushy cell to endure the silent treatment alone.

15

"WHY DO YOU HAVE to try so hard to piss him off?" Ethan growled when they reached the seducers level.

"Ethan, you know that's my favorite hobby." Gypsy winked at him as they exited the elevator in stride with each other.

"Yeah, I know." Ethan pulled out a pair of goggles that were dark enough to pass for sunglasses. "You really are screwed up. You know that, right?" He slipped the goggles on.

"Is that your professional analysis, Doctor?" Gypsy asked as she put on her own goggles.

"My professional opinion is you shouldn't push Danato's buttons, because one of these days, he's going to fail your little tests."

"Oh, Ethan, that's the whole point." Gypsy didn't have to see his eyes to know they were tight slits.

They reached their designated cell and pulled out foam earplugs. The glass to the cell was artificially frosted over to protect them. Gypsy could see the shadow of their prisoner pacing inside, not far from the door. There was one small spot on the glass where the frost had been scratched away, revealing translucent glass that was dangerous to anyone who might be stupid enough to peer through it. "Danato is a good man, Gypsy. When are you going to finally trust him?" Ethan slipped in one ear plug.

"I do trust him." She slipped in one of her earplugs. "Geez, Ethan, you really don't get this game, do you?" She slipped in her other plug.

"You really don't get how fucked up you are?" Ethan murmured low enough that he probably thought she couldn't hear him. She resisted the urge to express her complete understanding of her psychological issues with or without his help, but her amusement with the conversation had long since passed and she didn't want to deprive him of his ever-valued last word.

Once their earplugs and goggles were secured, they opened the cell to transfer their prisoner. The serpentine creature within would have appeared to be a beautiful woman or man to anyone not wearing safety goggles. To them, it just looked like a giant cobra with human arms and emerald eyes.

Without the earplugs, the screech the creature emitted would have translated into a beautiful song that could lure anyone as easily as a rat to the pied piper. As it was, the screech still held a melodious undertone that begged to be paid attention to.

They restrained the prisoner by either arm and dragged it to an adjacent cell that was properly etched so it couldn't be scratched off. Ethan proceeded inside the cell with the creature alone. He didn't need Gypsy's help, but they never moved the siren by themselves. The desire to remove the earplugs was nearly overwhelming, even with the visual block.

Gypsy had often wondered how the siren would make itself appear to her. The creature relied on physical attraction to draw people in. She no longer desired any man, and she had never really had any attraction to women, so what would it lure her with?

Unable to resist her curiosity this time, she pulled off her goggles. She caught a view of a little girl with a teddy bear in hand, before Ethan pushed her away from the door and shut it behind him.

"What the hell are you doing?" he said, ripping out one of her plugs so she could hear him yell at full volume.

"Interesting," she said.

"Gypsy!" Ethan pulled out his own plugs and took his goggles off. He huffed and stammered, trying to find the words for his rebuke. She waited for his anger to simmer down, as it always did when she didn't offer any retaliation to keep it going. "What... what did it show you?"

"A child," she said.

"Really?" he said. "You think that would work on you?" he asked carefully, not trying to insult her maternal instincts, but at the same time very surprised that she might actually have them.

"She had a teddy bear," she added.

"Oh." Ethan nodded as if that was the clincher in the portrait of seduction. He smiled at her. She didn't like that smile. It was honest enough, but it came with a flicker of interest in her beyond friendship. Ethan knew she wasn't interested in him, or any man, in that way, but her tenacity occasionally drew his attraction. When it wasn't pissing him off, that is.

"You want to take a peek?" she asked. "I won't tell."

Ethan's amusement faded as he debated indulging in that temptation. He looked at the cell and then back at her. "Nah," he said almost somberly, "I already know what I would see. I'm pretty predictable in that department." He chucked her shoulder and headed out ahead of her.

16

IT WASN'T UNTIL HER bland, prisoner-worthy meal, and the glimpse of the dusking sky through the skylights, that Cori realized they were actually going to make her spend the night in prison. She was certainly not a rookie at occupying the facility she was supposed to be employed at, but somehow she'd still thought a certain urgency or priority would be taken with her.

She had made some leeway with Danato, at least in letting her see Cleos, but after the fire incident, she could hardly blame him for tightening the leash on his generosity. Her rings were going back and forth between being problematic and helpful. So far, they had been problematic, and she was debating whether or not to make them helpful again.

An electronic number pad similar to the elemental cells upstairs locked and unlocked the door. It was a faulty design, since Efrat could always fry them and escape his confines to roam the prison freely. Since she still had his power in her rings, there was no reason not to apply the same tactic.

Technically, she would be escaping. That meant she was risking being caught, which meant any progress she was gaining toward convincing Danato of who she was would be lost.

At this point, Danato was leery of her. Belus was distrustful. Ethan was indifferent, and she wasn't sure what Gypsy thought of her, but it was a good guess that she didn't really have a friend there.

Cori cursed and pitted her frustrations into the door. It was hard to call up the power without the fear that usually accompanied it, but she knew it was just about concentration. It had always been about concentration, but the elementals had been given too much power too fast. They hadn't had the mental capacity to focus that much power, let alone stop it when their emotions flared.

The bolt she released was smaller than she intended, but it did the trick. She saw sparks through the small window in the door and the door clicked open.

She padded through the hall to the nurse's station. Two nurses were on duty, one was reading a magazine and popping bubbles with her gum, and the other was painting her toenails. Cori wondered if she should have been a nurse instead of a horticulturist. Maybe she wouldn't be searching for a genie in a schism of her own life path.

She hadn't really planned out what to do after she left the cell. She could certainly attack the women and knock them out, but she wasn't sure if they had an alarm button.

If she could sneak out rather than galvanize the entire prison, she would have more time to deal with the genie.

Cori took advantage of the preoccupied women and slunk across the floor on her hands and knees. Once she was at the circular counter station, she leaned against the base. The main entrance was through a short field of clear glass that was considered a waiting area. Even if she could sneak to it, she still had to get out unnoticed.

A man's voice sounded from down the hall behind the hub station. It was most likely one of the doctors, since he managed to convey pomposity with a simple greeting. Cori grimaced at her fabulous luck. She didn't want to make a snap decision, so she just did nothing. The man stopped at the hub to flirt with the ladies, who were more than happy to oblige with sultry responses and ear-grating giggles. His white tennis shoes and blue scrub pants were in view, but the overhang of the counter ledge kept the rest of him hidden.

Cori tucked her legs in a little more and rethought the situation. She could have knocked out the two women with ease, but she wasn't sure about the doctor. At any rate, three against one was a bet she wasn't willing to risk with her fluctuating skills.

She waited while the three conversed. She had hoped they might all sneak off to an examination room for a three-way, but propriety and common decency were working against her.

When she'd had enough of the cheeky laughter and benign small talk, Cori concentrated her energy on the doctor's pant hem. She tried to imagine she was trying to burn a tiny ant with a magnifying glass on a sunny day, and not trying to set a man's pants on fire, since a fireball might have been noticeably abnormal.

Eventually, the fabric of his pants started to smolder, wafting smoke up his leg. The conversation turned to comments about the smell, and Cori geared up for her escape. Just as the man's pants produced a flame, he discovered the source and started yelling and dancing around. The women screamed and one of them yelled for him to stop, drop, and roll as children are taught in school. Of course, no one ever tells you it's going to hurt like a bitch when you do.

The nurse leaped over the counter and pushed the doctor down. Cori was nearly discovered twice. The first time by the woman patting down his leg in front of her—only a slight turn of her head would have put Cori in her peripheral vision. The second time she nearly ran into the other nurse's legs when she whipped around the counter announcing that she was going to get a burn kit.

Cori crawled, apelike, to the front entrance and slipped out, worming her way by the windows until she was completely out of view. She debated on the elevator, and decided that the stairs were always the wisest option, or at least the most reliable. Stairs were not her favored method of transport, but the elevators had a mind of their own and found it unnecessary to make fast ascents or descents during any crisis.

She took the single flight with ease and peered out the window on the main level. She didn't see anyone. The cafeteria was closed for the night, and the dock would have minimal staff, if any. Assuming Danato was not in his office for a late night, and Ethan wasn't in the gym working out, she was in the clear to get to the prop room without any impromptu interruptions.

She snuck down the hall, past the darkened gym, and into the prop room. She flicked on the humming fluorescent lights that might as well have been night lights with as much illumination as they offered. She slipped through the piles of valuable, powerful, dangerous crap until she reached the area she had been in when the lamp got disturbed. She searched with her eyes, being careful not to disturb anything else. She soon found the snow globe, but no lamp.

"Shit, where is it?" she whispered to herself.

"Looking for this?" Danato's voice shocked her erect, and she bumped the snow globe off its pile. She caught it before it could break and add more trouble to her to do list.

Danato stood at the doorway with the lamp she was looking for hanging carefully by the crook of his finger. She gripped the snow globe like a baseball. The fleeting thought of throwing the decoration at him passed, and she replaced it on the pile carefully.

If Ethan or Gypsy had stood in the doorway, she might have attempted a grandiose battle or at least a heated negotiation for the return of it, but she couldn't fight Danato. His strength was the obvious deterrent, but she just couldn't bring herself to disrespect him in that way.

Danato seemed to recognize that. The glower that should have been painted on his face changed to calm indifference. Whether he was actually calm or just building up for a proper explosion, she wasn't sure. He lowered the lamp. "We moved the lamps while you were occupied with Gypsy and Ethan. We suspected you would try this."

Cori bit her lips back and nodded. She continued to underestimate Danato. The safety of the prison was always his first priority, and that would never change. "Of course." She looked at her feet. She had practically walked right into this trap. Actually, that was exactly what she had done. He had been testing her, and she had failed.

"Come to my office when you're done. Don't forget to shut the lights off." He left, shutting the door behind him. Cori looked around the room for a hole to crawl into, but since one was not readily available, she decided to go collect her punishment.

No one jumped her outside the room. There were no guards in the foyer to make sure she didn't escape. Danato expected her to comply with his request. She wanted to believe it was because he was starting to trust her, but it was more likely because he knew he had what she wanted and she wouldn't leave without it.

She raised her hand to open the door, but she decided to knock. Danato waved her in, barely looking up from his paperwork. The lamp was sitting on the edge of his desk as if it was a bowl of sweets universally offered to anyone comfortable enough to take candy from a stranger.

She closed the door behind her and sat down in front of his desk. She didn't want to show too much interest in the lamp, but she couldn't help but observe the intricate writing on it. She had hardly afforded it a glance the first time she had seen it. She had been naïve to think she was done with it when she'd walked away from it the first time.

"The inscription isn't instructions," Danato said.

"Pardon?" Cori said, drawing her attention back to him.

His eyes peered over his glasses, only momentarily offering his attention before he went back to work. "The inscription is a spell, or curse, if you prefer. It binds the genie to the lamp. That..." He nodded to the lamp. "...is his prison."

"Danato... I..." She started to apologize even though she knew it wouldn't help.

"How many wishes have you used?" he said abruptly, leaning back in his chair.

"Umm, well... I'm not sure. I wished for things to go back to normal. Since then, I've wished to undo my wish about a dozen times."

"You get three wishes. Those wishes are connected to you and contingent upon nothing. If you had any wishes left when you wished to undo your wishes, then that should have worked, albeit with some lasting repercussions."

"It didn't work, though. I'm still nobody to you."

"That means all three wishes were used by the time you made that wish."

"But I didn't."

"You did," Danato said more firmly, as if that would suddenly make her change her mind. "Think back," he said in a softer tone as he leaned back in his chair. The chair squawked in objection but maintained his large frame. "You must have wished twice before that wish. You could have said it in a dream and it still would have counted."

"A dream?" Cori asked. Danato nodded. She furrowed her brow, trying to remember the first time she would have made a wish. "I..."

"Yes?" Danato leaned forward just slightly.

Cori groaned and put her head down. "It was outside of my real timeline. I thought it didn't count."

"Timeline?"

"Long story, the rings again." She waved her fingers.

"What did you wish for?"

"I wished that you could have a better employee than me." Cori chuckled. "I guess that would be Gypsy." Danato didn't join her, but he probably recognized that she wasn't laughing from humor.

"What was the second wish?"

Cori sighed and shrugged. "I don't remember."

"It's been activated already. Think, Cori. Genies interpret things literally. For example, your version of normal and the genie's were very different, weren't they?"

Cori nodded. "My mother was still alive. I just finished college and was engaged to some guy. It was what I used to imagine my future to be, before..." She frowned and exhaled. Danato waited for her to verbalize her epiphany. "I wished that I had never come here. I was referring to... oh, son of a... He took me back to life without the prison, and then stuck me in my future version of normal." Cori shook her head. "I've used all three wishes."

She slumped back in her chair. Her eyes were watering, but she felt stressed more than sad. It had never occurred to her that she might be stuck with her wish—wishes. "I'm stuck here, aren't I?"

She could see Danato debate on how to respond. She laughed, letting one or two tears out before she got control of them. "You don't know how honest to be. Despite what you think of me, I'm tougher than I appear. If I can't change things back, just tell me. As much as I love all of you, I would rather go back to my mother and get to know my new fiancé than live a life that is persistently two steps left of where it should be."

When Danato still didn't answer, she assumed the worst and fought back the pain of his indifference. She stood up, clearing her throat of the lump that would prevent her from appearing composed. "With your permission, I'll leave on the next truck. I won't bother you again." She moved to the door, hoping against hope that he would stop her, but her hand hit the knob without any objection.

Cori twisted the knob and pulled, but the door didn't budge. She pulled harder, assuming it had only stuck, but she couldn't move it. She turned back to Danato for an explanation, but he seemed rather surprised by the immobile entrance. "Have a seat," he said, trying to hide his surprise by burying his head in paperwork.

She complied while Danato fiddled with his pencil. He was probably deep in thought, but his eyes were resting firmly on her. "I want to help you, Cori." He said it with finality, but she still waited for the qualifier to follow. She wasn't sure what he could do to help, or what she could say to sway him further onto her side. "I don't entirely trust you, but only because I believe you. I've been tricked before. You have to understand that the power that genies possess is nearly infinite. They are contained deities. If your rings were to absorb that power…"

Cori shook her head. "No, I don't think it works that way… at least, not so far. The power must be tangible. Daniel McGrath used his power on me—"

"Daniel McGrath?" Danato tensed.

"Don't worry I definitely didn't absorb that. The power must be tangible."

"Perhaps, but you are preventing the genie's power from working on you."

"What do you mean? I'm here, aren't I?"

Danato leaned forward. "Cori, the reason we are reluctant to believe you are the victim of a genie is because you *know* you are a victim. You shouldn't remember your old life, just as we don't remember you. Something—I assume it is those rings—is preventing you from forgetting."

"Maybe it's not the rings. Cleos put a block in my mind to prevent anyone from hypnotizing me. Maybe somehow it's preventing me from forgetting." Danato didn't argue with that point, but he didn't acknowledge that she might be right. He just continued to battle his own thoughts. "I know you have a duty, Danato, but I'm telling you the truth. I don't know what else to do to convince you."

"I told you I believe you. I just don't trust you."

"You don't have to trust *me*. Just trust your instincts. Put away the rule book. I know you want to. Tell me... is there a way to undo my wishes?"

Danato paused, debating the last vestiges of his protocol. "Yes."

Cori clapped her hands together and held them to her mouth. She released the tension she had been holding and pushed away the emotions that wanted to replace it. She wanted to jump across the desk and hug Danato, but for obvious reasons, she resisted. "Then please, help me return to my not-so-normal life."

"I..." His voice trailed off and his eyes moved behind her. The door to the office opened and Cori's enthusiasm for their progress waned even before Belus came into her view.

Belus looked between them and then at the lamp. He was usually a reserved man, without an obvious opinion on his face, but he didn't seem to be able to hide his disapproval of her. Cori wondered why looking like Danato's dead wife, drove ire into his eyes.

"Why is she still here?" Belus asked, as if she weren't in the room. Cori looked away from them, giving them the privacy required to have a conversation about her behind her back.

"She is still here because I am asking her the questions that you didn't this afternoon."

"This is a waste of time. She needs to be contained," Belus spat.

"What do you suggest?" Danato lowered his voice even more, so it sounded like distant thunder instead of a whisper. "The only way to contain her with those powers is to put her up with the elementals."

Cori's tension returned, but she resisted every instinct to beg against that prospect. She needed to let Danato defend her. Belus would still follow Danato's orders, even if he didn't agree with them. Her contributions, on the other hand, would only make the argument leading to that conclusion more arduous.

"We can put a single guard on her with an elemental weapon," Belus suggested. Danato sat back in his chair. He wasn't so much contemplating the suggestion as giving

Belus a chance to reconsider his perspective before they ended up in a full-scale argument. Belus must have sensed he was on losing ground, even with his insistence. "What do *you* suggest we do?"

"I think it's time we got to the bottom of this once and for all."

"I thought we were waiting for the medical report."

Danato didn't so much roll his eyes as blink away his lassitude from the conversation. "She's human, Belus. Can we move on? I know why you are fighting this so hard, and I appreciate that protection, but I think *you* are now the one getting distracted by her resemblance."

Belus looked at her, and she caught his eye before looking away. He seemed to be accusing her of something, but it faded until something of his normal demeanor returned. Danato recognized the change as well. "Good. Now, let's talk to the genie."

17

ORI WASN'T SURE WHAT she'd expected to happen when Danato pulled the lid off the lamp. Perhaps she'd thought the genie would announce his presence with a grand, impossibly echoing voice and demand a reason for his summons. She certainly wasn't prepared for his smoky form to solidify in the chair next to her with a pile of scrolls—that, despite his phenomenal cosmic power, required him to wear a magnifying monocle to read.

Tattoos mirroring the lamp's etchings covered his bald head and shirtless torso. She started to understand what Danato meant by him being imprisoned. Judging by the sheer number of tattoos—which covered every bit of his exposed skin—she had to assume that he was being secured by a very powerful spell. In turn, that led her to conclude the man sitting beside her, reading his scrolls as if it were a commonplace event, may have been the most powerful being in the entire prison, save... no one.

She gulped at that thought. She had been so wrapped up in her ordeal with Efrat at the time, she hadn't even considered him a threat. Now she wasn't sure she even wanted to proceed with negotiating with him for fear of how much worse he could make her life.

Sensing her eyes on him, he looked over at her for the first time. She didn't want to be openly staring at him, but she couldn't help it. He saw her trancelike fear and smiled. It wasn't the manic leer of a deviant mind, nor was it the cocksure sneer of a man proud of his accomplishments; it was just a smile. That perplexed her even more, but when she opened her mouth to speak to him, he returned to his scrolls.

"Cori." Danato's voice was quiet. When she looked at him, he gave her a stare that said she shouldn't be gawking at a man capable of destroying her with a snap of his fingers. She sat back in her chair and tried to reduce the number of glances she offered him. She could see Belus eyeing her between chapters in the large, overly earmarked book he had fetched from the file cabinet. She closed her eyes and focused on the ticking clock. She was really starting to appreciate that clock.

"Here we are," Belus announced finally. "We are requesting the stipulations on resignation of all three successive wishes regarding... state your full name." Belus and Danato looked up at her from the large book. She sputtered before stating it clearly, as if she were on trial.

"Corinthia Ellen Reiger," Belus repeated it to finish his request properly. "We would also like to know the outcome of her resignation of wishes regarding us."

The genie chuckled. "You know I can't tell you that. Her past, present, and future are currently bound under the terms of the wishes. Once she relinquishes those wishes, she will return to her previous present, which will rewrite her to *her* original past, and place her in line with *her* intended future. I have no obligation to tell you what that is, nor how it impacts anyone else."

"But you know," Danato pointed out.

"Of course I know." The genie looked at her before returning his attention to them. "But I can no more tell you her future than you can walk through walls." He gestured toward his body, as if that stipulation were written on him, which it probably was. "Perhaps you could ask me a simple question, one that isn't strictly forbidden to answer."

Danato and Belus exchanged a look. "Is she who she says she is?" Danato asked, glancing at her. She turned to the genie, just as intrigued at hearing the answer as they were.

The genie locked eyes with her. She felt small sitting next to him, even though he wasn't particularly tall. He was well-muscled and a good deal paler than she remembered him being. The tattoos on his face had beautiful sharp black lines. She raised her hand to touch his face. He didn't stop her, but she stopped just short of actually touching him.

"Yes," the genie spoke, breaking her concentration. "She is who she says." There seemed to be a sigh of relief in the room.

"I thought I couldn't be hypnotized or mesmerized anymore," she said, still locked in his eyes.

He leaned in just a little. "You aren't bewitched. You're just reacting to seeing my corporeal form." He lowered his voice. "I'm as close to a god as the Earth allows, and you can't help but be drawn to me."

"Is that why you usually stay translucent?"

"Mm-hmm."

She gulped. "Can I touch you?"

"Cori!" Danato's rebuke ended her fixation. She tucked her hands under her arms. She was aware of how childish it looked, but she didn't know how else to keep herself from reaching out to the man next to her. She was reasonably terrified of him, but for some reason she desired to touch his skin.

"Don't worry," the genie whispered. "They feel it too. They are just better at fighting it."

"What are the stipulations of release?" Belus asked, getting them back on task.

"The stipulations are the standard 1-2-3 clause," the genie said, pulling out a new scroll. Belus flipped through his own plague of Post-It notes to find the clause. After a quick read, he looked up at her. She raised a brow, offering the question she knew didn't need to be asked. "Is that the only offer?"

"That stipulation will dissolve all three wishes, and null her current recent past, and erase this present in lieu of hers."

"Is that what you want? To be rid of this version of normal?" Danato asked her. She could see the sympathy in his eyes, and at first she didn't understand why. As it dawned on her, she felt her heart clench.

"If I dissolve all three wishes, I lose my mother again." It wasn't really a question so much as an acknowledgement, so they knew she knew what the ramifications of the choice were. Danato nodded.

Despite being committed to her decision just seconds before the statement, she wondered if she was being selfish in choosing a particular path in life over her mother's very existence. Shouldn't she be willing to give up her adoptive family—who were apparently just fine without her—for her blood family?

18

CORI STOOD OUTSIDE OF the office in clear view of the window. She had stepped out to clear her mind and give herself a chance to make an honest decision. To her surprise, Belus had let her leave the room; however, she assumed he was watching her like a hawk.

She knew that her mother being alive was a complete tangent to her history, but now that she had her back, she wasn't sure she wanted to let her go. On the other hand, she couldn't have it both ways. She was either going to go back to life as it was and lose her mother, or she was going to have to choose between a life with her mom and a fiancé she didn't know, or people she knew, but who didn't know her.

Even as things were now, she wasn't sure Belus or Danato would let her stay. She may not have the option of trying to recreate a life here. Ethan didn't appear to be the same man she loved, so maybe that was for the best.

She leaned against the wall and tried to rationalize that her mother had been dead before, and she had accepted it, eventually. However, she wasn't sure she could accept it when she was the one causing her to die.

"This is bullshit," she said when Danato stepped into the hall to check on her.

"Yes, I know," he said with the only level of softness his voice was capable of.

"I shouldn't have to decide my mother's fate like this. It's too much to ask!"

"I know," he said again. He didn't seem to have any better answers for her.

"I know what I have to do. I knew it before I came here, but... she's my mother," she said with more anger than sadness.

Danato nodded. "Yes, I can't imagine how hard this is for you, but..." He paused. "Perhaps you should hear the conditions of the resignation before you commit one way or another. I don't know that it will make your decision easier, but at least it will be informed."

"Why do I keep screwing things up?" She wanted to punch a wall, but she knew it would only hurt, so she settled on thumping it with the meaty part of her fist. "I have been in and out of trouble since I got here! I should just rid you of myself for good and go back to my mother. You would be none the wiser, and I doubt very much anyone would miss me."

Danato nodded. She thought he was agreeing with her, which made her turn away to shield herself from the slight. "I'm going to skip the part where I tell you that I wouldn't be able to let you leave with your rings still functional. Instead, I'm going to ask you what your Danato would say to your leaving."

Cori turned back to see if he was saying it to get her to think about it, or if he really wanted to know. His pause gave her the opening to answer. "Danato would be torn between letting me be with my mother and keeping me here with him. He would probably hide behind his duty to the secrecy of the prison, so I would have to stay, rather than appear to rule for his own preferences."

"And what would your Ethan think of you giving up your life with him for your mother?"

Cori sighed. She missed Ethan so much. Even with his likeness being so close, she felt farther from him than Danato and Belus. At least they were essentially the same men, but Ethan was different. He had matured differently. Slower or quicker, she wasn't sure which. At any rate, he was not hers and she knew he never would be. "Ethan is my rock. Without him... there's just too much history to lose. I need him."

"Mothers are always intended to be left behind so the children can start their own lives," Danato said. "That doesn't negate your love or your connection. It just means you are continuing with the life that she gave you."

Cori wasn't sure she felt less guilty about signing her mother's death certificate, but she preferred that Danato agreed with her. The only logical choice was the only practical choice as well.

"Come back in so we can discuss the stipulations. You'll have time to make your final decision."

B ACK IN THE OFFICE, Cori didn't feel compelled to touch the genie anymore. She wasn't sure if it was because of the blunt edge of the situation, or if he had adjusted his form so as not to distract her.

She thought back to her first encounter with him and tried to think if she could have done anything different to prevent this from happening. If she made it back to her original life, she was going to yet again have to explain herself.

"You know," Cori said, bringing everyone out of their reading. "I didn't technically rub the lamp. I kicked it with my shoed foot."

No one jumped for joy at the admission like she had hoped. "The contract between the lamp and the wisher is activated by touch on the body of the lamp," Belus recited, as if he was familiar with the passage that defined the activation. "If the material that touches the lamp is considered clothing—gloves, shoes, etcetera—it is an extension of the body and counts as interaction. You could, however, place the lamp inside of a bag or purse and carry it without activating, as long as all tangible handling, clothed or otherwise, remained on the handle or spout."

"Oh," Cori said, disappointed by the exceptional detail in the genie laws.

"Cori," Danato began, "we need to explain the 1-2-3 clause to you before you decide anything. In order to relinquish your wishes and go back to your version of reality, you must endure sacrifices."

"That doesn't sound appealing."

"You can choose one, two, or three sacrifices, but obviously the lower number requires the greatest detriment," Danato explained.

"Okay," she said, bracing herself for the hard truth. "Let's have it."

"One death, two accidents, or three minor inconveniences," Danato summed up.

"What does that mean?" Cori asked Danato, but he turned to Belus. Belus looked at her. She raised her eyebrow in expectation.

"Choosing only one debt for the favor of releasing you means that someone you know must die," Belus said.

Cori shrugged. "My mother will die if I do this, anyway."

"Unfortunately," Belus said, "that doesn't count, since she was within the boundary of the wish. Someone else you know will die."

"Who?" she asked, even though she already knew it wasn't an option.

"That's the nature of the sacrifice. You don't know who," Danato interjected. "It could be your ninety-year-old third-grade teacher, or it could be... one of us."

Cori felt her supper rise in her throat. She shook her head and swallowed the acidity back to her stomach. "No way, I won't risk that. No one gets to die because of me."

Both Danato and Belus seemed to ease upon hearing that. She wasn't sure if it was officially a test of her character, but she knew that would always be a test she could pass. "The other option is two accidents," Belus continued. "This usually involves others, but it can be you."

"What kind of accidents?"

"It can be car accidents, work-related accidents, or just household accidents, but it won't cause death."

"That doesn't sound too horrible," Cori said, scooting to the edge of her chair in anticipation of finding a solution to her problem. "What are we talking: bruises, broken bones?"

"Yes," Belus said, glancing at Danato, which meant it was worse than she was interpreting, "but it could also mean head trauma resulting in comas, spinal injuries resulting in paralysis. It excludes death, but it doesn't mean all your limbs have to be intact and functional."

Cori shot a look at the genie, who seemed rather bored with the conversation. She wondered if it was his decision that created these potentially life-changing sacrifices, or if his actions were just as bound as his body. "And I'm sure I don't get to choose who. I mean, not that it would be worth the risk of lifelong handicap parking, but I do have a few enemies." She smiled to let them know she was joking, but neither of them found her amusing and they seemed genuinely concerned that she would consider this path, so she moved on. "Door number three?"

"Three minor inconveniences," Belus said. "Unlike the others, these can only happen to you."

"That's good," she said, more hopeful than enthusiastic.

"Yes, if you are willing to take them on, but..." Belus paused, looking her over.

"What?" she said, irritated by his dramatic pauses. She knew he was only doing it to skip the repetitive and verbose heeds to caution, but it was damned annoying.

"As it is stated, the inconveniences are minor because they don't cause injury or death to you or others around you, but they can cause incidental harm." Belus paused again, not so much for drama, but to let her comprehend the statement. "A minor inconvenience to you might be your coat zipper breaking, but the result of the inconvenience might be that you are unprotected by the elements and freeze to death. The zipper breaking, of course, is minor, but since you are unprepared to compensate, other circumstances can lead you to bigger problems."

"I could drop a bucket of water, and an electrical wire could fall in the puddle and roast me?"

Belus offered the genie a glance as he yawned. "He won't intentionally try to kill you, but if you agree to the three inconveniences, you must understand that they will probably cause a greater failure later on. It's just how it works. They are sacrifices, after all."

"When will the inconveniences occur?"

"Over the course of the remainder of your life," Belus said sympathetically.

"Oh, for crap's sake! Like I need another threat looming over my head."

"You will know after each inconvenience occurs. That is one of the written rules."

"If I agree to this..." Cori looked at the genie for her answer. "If I agree to my debts, what exactly happens?"

He smiled at her, and again, it was an honest smile. "The option to renege on your current fortunes in exchange for your misfortunes will expire in 48 hours. After that, you will permanently be placed in this life with no option to return to your other life. If you agree, simply hold the lamp by the spout and handle and say, 'Genie, I accept your offer' and I will send you back to your former life: Gypsy will no longer be employed here, and your path of normalcy with your mother and fiancé will be exchanged for your previous happy existence here at the prison."

20

"Y OU DON'T HAVE TO answer now, if you don't want to," Danato said when Cori hadn't looked up from her lap in over a minute. "You can stay at the house tonight and sleep on it. Give him your answer in the morning." She caught a glimpse in her periphery of the nonverbal debate that statement sparked, but in the end, Danato slammed his fist into the desk and Belus walked out.

She looked at the genie and scanned his tattooed spells. "Why?" she asked.

"Because I think a decision, this important should be given time, plus you look like you need some rest," Danato answered.

"I don't think that's what she's asking," the genie said, staring at Cori as hard as she was staring at him. "Why don't you step outside a moment, Danato?"

"I don't think so." The genie turned away from Cori and glowered at Danato. "You have no power here, genie, don't waste your lure."

"I have more than you think. Now go. I won't ask again."

Cori could *feel* his full form return more than she could see it. As far as her eyes could see, he was the same, but her heart raced and she felt the fear and attraction she had felt before. She was certain Danato could feel it too, because he left without another objection. He may not have been her Danato, but she was pretty sure it was against several protocols to leave someone alone in a room with an active genie.

When he turned back to look at her, the volume of his magnetism had reduced dramatically. He was either trying to make her more comfortable, or he intended to have an honest conversation with her. "You have something to say?"

"Why do you do this? All this scheming and turbulence?" she asked.

He leaned forward as if he was going to tell her a secret. She resisted the urge to lean in. "For the same reason that you take air into your lungs: because I have to." He motioned to his tattoos.

"Breathing is an involuntary response. If I don't breathe, I die, and I can't choose to not breathe. Even if I held my breath, I would just pass out and continue breathing normally in my unconscious state. Are you saying you have to do what you do because you have no choice, or because you don't like what the choice is?"

"Why are you asking me this?"

"Curiosity, I suppose, but mostly I think I just want to know if I should hate you or not."

"That is my prison." The genie nodded to the lamp on the desk. "The rules that I abide by are written in my scrolls. The scrolls are what you should hate. I am merely the enforcer designated to carry out those asinine things. And to answer your question, I do as the scrolls demand, because if I don't, I will be tormented."

"Torture?" Cori asked.

"Yes, though not in the form you might think. Pain is corporeal. The torture I receive is more... cerebral, but it is nonetheless torture."

"Why you? What did you do to deserve your prison?"

He chuckled. The sound was merriment and manliness combined. When he had finished, he settled his arm on the back of her chair and started stroking his fingers along her temple. The contact didn't feel flirtatious, but she got the sense that she should be flattered that he deemed her worthy of the gentle gesture.

"Have you ever caught a firefly in a jar?" he asked. She nodded and closed her eyes to concentrate on his touch. "You thought nothing of it, did you?"

"No, but I always let them go again."

"Fireflies only live long enough to mate and lay eggs. Hours inside a jar might seem like nothing to you, but an eternity to them."

"How long do you live?" Cori opened her eyes and saw that he had closed his as well. His almond eyes opened and met her gaze with an auburn iris that in the right light might have seemed red. Though he had no hair to speak of, she imagined he would look unjustly attractive with a mop of messy auburn waves to match his eyes.

"Death is corporeal, but I maintain sentient thought for over one thousand years."

Cori's mouth dropped open, not because of shock, but because she had too many competing questions, and she wasn't sure which one to start with. She pulled her leg up under her and leaned over the arm of her chair. His caress had since stopped, but at some point she'd stopped being so intent on receiving it. "What happens after one thousand? What were you before the thousand years?"

"I was not aware before, and I will not be aware after, but for now, I am aware, and I have control of my power."

Cori took in a breath. "What are you? You said you were as close to a god as Earth allows. Are you a demi-god?"

"I suppose that's as good a name as any."

"But why are you here? Why are you imprisoned? *How* are you being imprisoned? What's more powerful than a demi-god? Were you imprisoned by a god, the God, or was it the devil?"

He chuckled again. "I know not of gods and monsters," he said as if he were quoting a book. "I only know of men, and they are neither; but masquerade so well... as both."

Cori shook her head in vain, trying to make the conclusion she had come to go away. She stood and grabbed the lamp. She was careful to touch only the handle of it, but she was pretty certain that until her situation was settled, she would not be subject to any more wishes.

She examined the text on it. At first glance, she had assumed it was Arabic, but only because she had watched Aladdin too many times growing up. A closer inspection would have left her assuming Egyptian, but there weren't any birds or dog-headed figures. She racked her brain for the owner of the only other pictographic language she could think of.

She looked back at him. "This is Sumerian, isn't it?" The twinge of surprise on his face answered the question. "How the hell could men bind a demi-god to Earth?"

"As I said, I was not self-aware prior to my thousand years. The Sumerians were very talented conjurers. I was bound to that lamp long before I was ever aware of my own existence."

Cori carefully set down the lamp again. "Why?"

"Have we come full circle or are we still answering your original question?"

Cori sat back down beside him. "Why would they do this to you? What was their purpose?"

"Because they could. I may be powerful now, but once upon a time I was just a firefly—a very powerful firefly."

"But the scrolls are so definitive and vindictive. Why would they devise such turmoil?"

"Those scrolls are literal interpretations of fluid concepts. My imprisonment was designed to offer rain in times of drought, fertility to the barren, and health to the sick. 5,000 years ago, you would not have thought twice about sacrificing one life to sustain your crop and feed hundreds. Had you need, you might be willing to risk injury to two people so you could bear a child. And to heal the sick, three minor inconveniences are nothing. Nature demands balance, and for every wish there is a sacrifice."

"But I don't *want* my wishes! Why do I have to pay my sacrifice?"

The genie crinkled his nose. "That's where the literal text starts to get tangled with modern day scruples. At the time that I was bound, the Sumerians didn't ask for things as frivolous as wealth and fame; they wanted food, water, and health for their entire kingdom. The text interprets seeking wishes for individuals without dire need as narcissistic and gluttonous, therefore three sacrifices are inflicted without wishes being granted because you are considered unworthy. You did not intentionally seek me out, but you were in a need of help, so, therefore, the wishes were granted."

"Even though I didn't want them or ask for them."

"That's where the scope of my power as a sentient being and the decisive nature of the text start to be counterproductive. You were not granted three wishes accompanied by sacrifices, as the Sumerians were. You were bestowed three blessings. It's because you didn't ask for them that you did not have to sacrifice for them. However, since I am not an intuitive being by nature, I don't know what you want unless you specifically ask for it. That leaves me to grant wishes that you may not really want, or, in your case, devising my own interpretations from vague statements."

"Why does undoing the blessings mean I get punished?"

"In your text, it's referred to as the mollycoddle clause. It is designed to punish the ingrates. Returning blessings isn't really considered polite."

"Oh." Cori lowered her head, feeling sheepish about considering the wishes as a burden. It obviously took a great deal of power to make someone come back from the dead and change the path of her life. She shouldn't have taken that for granted. "Sorry."

The genie tipped his head, eyeing her carefully. "I don't take offense to you wanting to go back to your old life. It is your choice to make. I do wish that I could make the change without the sacrifices, but alas, genies don't get to rub their own lamps." He winked at her and she tried not to smile too big at his humor, since she didn't know if it was an intentional or incidental innuendo.

Cori looked over at the lamp and back at him. "So, how long are you stuck to the lamp?"

"My servitude will expire long after my sentient years have passed."

Cori frowned, mortified to hear this. Her reaction seemed to amuse him, but he didn't laugh. Instead, he twisted his finger around in her hair. She wasn't sure what the rules were regarding contact between him and his wishers, but she was getting the distinct impression that he hadn't spent this much time with a flesh-and-blood human in a while... or ever.

"So, your entire sentient life will be spent fulfilling wishes."

"I know nothing more."

"Can't someone just wish you free like in the movies?"

"No, it doesn't work quite like that."

"But there is a way?" she asked, and he nodded, combing his fingers through her hair. "What is it?"

"I can't tell you." He motioned to his tattooed spells again. "Against the rules. I can't tell you how to free me. All I can do is answer your questions or not."

"Great, another riddle to solve."

He chuckled at her and brushed his hand across her forehead. "You don't really want to free me, do you? I'm an earth-bound sentient demi-god. I could devour your free will like candy, even in this state. Imagine what I could do with freedom."

"What do you mean, devour my free will?"

His aura changed tangibly, and Cori felt the awesome power she had felt from him before. It was even stronger than before, and she could feel herself gravitating toward him uncontrollably. She reached to his tattoo-filled chest, but he grabbed her hand and pulled it back.

"Careful, they're sticky."

She looked up at him for further explanation. Her eyes locked, and she understood fully what he meant about free will. He would only need to ask, and she would have done anything. Not *anything* meaning offering herself to him or killing for him—though she would have done that too. She would have done *anything,* meaning she would have cut her own hand off and eaten it. That was too much power for any sentient being to possess for any amount of time.

There was only the tiniest sliver of hope left inside of her to think otherwise. That was the part of her that was still cognizant enough to realize that he wasn't actually asking her to *do* anything, despite having her fully under his influence.

His aura shifted again and his presence reduced back down to resistible levels. "See? I would be a terrible burden on this world."

Cori shook her head. "I disagree." His eyes widened with surprise. "You aren't human, so you aren't predisposed to being greedy and selfish. You aren't a wizard, so you aren't guaranteed to be an ass. I think you would have to abide by the same basic principles of balance as you do now. If you were the one choosing to make the changes, then you would have to choose the consequences. I think once you got a taste of the eye-for-an-eye, karma's-a-bitch lifestyle, you wouldn't get too carried away."

"Interesting theory, though I still doubt you would want to free me if you knew what it entailed, so there is no point in debating it. Have you made up your mind about the present offer?"

"I think I'll sleep on it, like Danato suggested."

"Very well. You know where to find me." The genie turned translucent in preparation for his return to the lamp.

"Wait, what's your name?" she asked, partially as an afterthought to her debate about offering him a farewell handshake since she probably wouldn't have this opportunity to speak with him ever again.

He smiled broadly and more roguishly than he had so far. "Some call me Rumpelstiltskin, but that's not my real name."

She wanted to inquire further about the meaning of that, but he was a wisp of smoke reversing into the lamp before she could.

"**Y**OU'VE GOT TO BE kidding me!" Gypsy slammed the door to the home office as hard as she could on her exit. The lights flickered in derision for the act. "What?" She threw up her arms at the house. "That's what doors are for! If you don't want me to slam doors, then don't form as a house!"

"Gypsy," Ethan said from the kitchen as the lights glowed a little too brightly before dimming back to normal. "Don't take it out on the house."

"I can't believe they're bringing her back here." Gypsy grabbed a bottle of water from the fridge and hopped onto the counter to chug it.

"I'm not very happy about it either," he said as he worked on cutting up the last veggies for his stir fry.

"Bull shit, you aren't," she said after catching a breath from her drink. He offered her a confused look. "Oh, come on. That ought to be the easiest lay you'll ever get. She's already your wife."

"She's not my wife," he grumbled.

"*She* thinks she is. Just butter her up with a little chivalry and she'll put out. Trust me, I know the type.

She'll pretend to be hard to get, but just hint at the prospect of living happily ever after, and she'll spread wide and high."

Ethan shook his head at her vulgarity, but she could see his lip tugging into his cheek. "Do you believe her?" he asked, not looking at her.

"Do you?" she posed right back. He shrugged, not willing to give an answer before she gave hers. "I don't think disbelief is an option anymore. Let's face it, a genie can't be fooled. If he says she's telling the truth, then that's it. Lie detector test passed."

Ethan nodded. "Doesn't that bother you?" He continued to move his vegetables about, but she knew he was watching her from the corner of his eye.

"What, that I won't be here?" she asked, not really mentioning specifically what he was worried about. "You poor bastard. Think how bored you'll be without me." He smiled at that. She hopped off the counter and scooted in beside him. She could sense him tense against her. "Maybe we should finally knock one out before she sends me back." When he didn't readily respond to her, she grabbed his butt tightly.

"Gypsy, don't."

"Don't what? Doesn't that sound like a good idea?" She leaned in and smelled him. She knew it wouldn't take much to get him excited. Despite the image he presented, his experiences with women were few and far between.

"It always sounds like a good idea in theory, but in reality, you don't really want it." He looked at her without the yearning that she wanted. He looked at her with piteous sympathy. She wanted to laugh at him and continue with the ruse, but all she managed was a scoff.

"What are you, a eunuch?" she snarled before reaching to the front of his pants. He winced, but not out of pleasure; she was gripping too tightly for that. "No, you aren't."

"How far are you going to take this, Gypsy?" He lowered his voice to sound stern. "I'm not going to keep playing this game."

"What game?" she said innocently, relaxing her grip so she could return him to pleasure.

"It's the same bloody game as with Danato!" he yelled, though he made no attempts to back away from her hand. "You just won't rest until one of us finally hurts you. Do you even realize how truly masochistic you are?"

"I always thought of myself as a sadist." Ethan pulled her hand away, clamping it by the wrist tightly. She smiled broadly at him, which made him angrier. "You take it so seriously, Ethan." With some effort, she pulled her hand from his grip. "It's just a game."

"It's not a game. It's your life and one of these days you are going to have to accept that."

"Apparently not," she said, moving away from him. "Since I'll be dead as soon as Cori un-wishes her wishes."

"You don't know that for sure," Ethan said, almost snappish.

She leaned on the side of the island to view his desperate rationalization. She always felt bad for tormenting him, but she couldn't ever seem to help herself. The truth was, Ethan was right. She didn't want to actually have sex with him.

She hated seeing other people derive pleasure from each other. It was like seeing something that she should want, but couldn't enjoy once she had it. It was the revolving door left from her sexual trauma. It had taken Ethan a good while to figure it out, but now that he understood she could never be fixed, he knew not to engage her passing interests, since they were just that: passing.

Ethan understood her enough to put up with it, but her frustrations with the constant debate left her craving something more than sex. Somewhere in the mix of abuses she had endured prior to joining the prison, her lines of pleasure and pain had got a little convoluted. She called it a game, but it was more than that.

Her sudden change into a safe world left her constantly waiting for the other shoe to drop. She didn't crave the pain, but she did crave the bait leading to the pain. She wanted to know how far she could push Danato and Ethan before they would snap.

She never doubted that someday one of them or both would eventually up and hit her, but it wasn't the pain she was seeking. It was the anticipation and challenge of breaking their gallantry that fueled her. They both thought they were above it, and she wanted so badly to rip away those masks, and prove they weren't.

22

I T WAS SURREAL WALKING into her home without feeling welcome. Cori was happy that Danato was allowing her to stay at the house. There had been another heated discussion with Belus about it, but in the end, he had no choice but to concede. With the genie essentially backing her up, there wasn't a lot of room to deny her story. Making her stay in the prison would just be rude.

Belus accompanied them home for dinner. It was a rare thing for her to see Belus and Danato in the house together, but neither Ethan nor Gypsy seemed surprised by his presence. *Her* attendance, however, was met with silent disapproval. They didn't outright reject her like a heathen in a Puritan village, but they were far from inviting.

Cori wavered in the between space of the dining room and living room, trying to decide what to do. Gypsy was reading a comic book in the living room. It was an anime, which explained her current style. The more she looked at her, the more familiar her face looked. If she had met her, it was probably a long time ago and hardly worth mentioning.

Ethan was preparing dinner. He offered her a glance, but nothing that led her to believe she could attempt a conversation.

When Danato slipped out of the room to change, Cori joined Belus at the fireplace. "I shouldn't be here," she whispered so Gypsy wouldn't hear, even though she probably did.

Belus looked at her, confounded that she was even talking to him. "Why didn't you object when Danato was insisting that you come here?"

"Because I didn't want to spend another night in the prison."

"Another? You haven't even spent one."

Cori cringed, not wanting to explain anything more about her other life, since the ramifications here wouldn't exist after tomorrow. "The dream feeders are pretty cruel to me when I'm inside the time bubble overnight," she answered. Belus seemed to at least sympathize with that. "I know it's unorthodox to ask this, especially in this situation, but maybe I could stay with..." Cori couldn't quite finish the request to ask if she could stay at his house. She had actually never been inside his house. Not for reasons specifically unwelcoming, but there had just never been cause to go there.

Belus's eyes narrowed as he predicted what she was about to ask. She could see how even the hint of opening his home to her was distasteful to him. She wasn't sure what she was thinking when she started the sentence, but now with part of it out, she wanted to travel back in time five seconds and slap herself before she could open her mouth.

"Never mind, I'd rather be unwelcome in a house I know." She walked away before she could see Belus's reaction. She headed to the island and sat down on a stool. Ethan eyed her change of location circumspectly. "Can I help you with anything?" she asked, mostly just to break the silence.

Ethan only offered a head shake in return. It wasn't the resounding beginning of a dialogue she had hoped for and the longer the silence dragged out, the more she felt like a foreign exchange student trying to find someone to hang out with at lunch.

Cori fiddled with her rings while she waited for Danato to return. Right now, he was the only person who actually wanted her there. "How do those work?" Ethan asked.

She looked up at him, shocked to hear something resembling communication. Unfortunately, she was too preoccupied to understand what he was asking. He smirked a little at her. She probably looked as dumbfounded as she felt. "The rings," he clarified. "How do they work?"

"Oh," she said loudly before she adjusted her volume to match his casual tone. "They protect me from other beings' powers, and sometimes they absorb it. I discovered it during an encounter with an elemental, but I didn't really understand them until—well, I still don't fully understand them. I was..." She stopped short when she realized she had taken liberties with the conversation. He probably just wanted to know if she could hurt him.

"Where did you get them?" he asked, to her surprise.

"They were a gift from you... Ethan... my Ethan." She paused to see his reaction, but he was unfazed by the mention of his other self's actions. "He had them made from a wizard's gold necklace he took from the time bubble."

"What can you do? What powers do you have?" he asked as casually as he could, but it was in that calmness that she saw the interrogation forming.

She lowered her head, not wanting to show how disappointed she was. "Fire and electricity are the most common ones. They seem to have a mind of their own when I'm scared or angry, as you've seen. I also have ice and water power, but they are sporadic. I think I'm going to wash up before dinner." She pointed toward the bathroom. "If that's okay?" she mumbled as she slipped off the stool.

"What did I say?" he asked, obviously noticing her sudden disinterest in the conversation. She debated on pretending she hadn't heard him, but he sounded sincerely concerned.

"I'm not here to hurt any of you. I wish you could believe that."

"I do believe that," he said flatly. She paused, trying to figure out what to do next. "I was only curious about them. I've never seen such a thing. Do you know how they work, or rather why they work?"

Cori slipped back onto her stool. She was pretty sure this was still an interrogation, but it was the curious kind and not the plotting kind, so she was willing to continue. "If you look very close, there are inscriptions in the gold. I assume a spell transferred through the smelting process. Maybe something left from the wizards."

"So can anyone use them, or do they only work on you?"

"I don't actually know. I can't get them off." She showed him how her fingers slipped off the rings, despite her best efforts. "They don't budge."

Ethan nodded, contemplating the solution to that riddle. "Did they come as a set? When did you add the wedding ring?"

"At our..." Cori chuckled and shook her head in embarrassment. "At my wedding. He wouldn't let me have the last ring until I made it all the way down the aisle."

"Was he worried you would take the ring and run?" Ethan smiled.

"He just wanted to surprise me." Cori couldn't help but lock eyes with him. The mutual gaze might have lingered, but the stir fry demanded his attention.

Ethan transferred the main dish to a serving platter and announced the meal was ready. Everyone sat down to a meal of stir fry and an uncomfortable silence.

23

G YPSY COULDN'T HELP BUT find the entire scene diverting. Ethan was doing his best to avoid eye contact with Cori, who was sitting beside her, but when he thought no one was watching, he would sneak a peek at her. She could tell he was already contemplating being with her.

Belus was focused on eating, but what no one else noticed was the knife he had hidden in his boot. It didn't matter what the genie had said, he was prepared for anything. "Be prepared" was a Boy Scout motto, but Belus took his preparations to the next level of "Be paranoid."

Danato, on the other hand, seemed to be completely enamored with the woman, and was sneaking in just as many glances as the horny young man beside him. Gypsy chuckled out loud at the thought of Danato and Ethan competing for the same woman. She was pretty sure Danato knew where to draw the line on inappropriate relationships, but it was still a funny image.

Cori looked over at her. "Something funny?" she asked.

Gypsy smirked at her. Naturally, Cori thought her amusement was somehow about her. "Nothing you would find amusement in. My humor tends to be a little dark."

"Oh," Cori said. It was all she could say. Gypsy had a knack for scaring off small talk.

"So, when do you plan on killing me?" she blurted out after Cori had taken a large bite of her meal. The mouths previously masticating happily sputtered, froze in shock, swallowed half-chewed food, and choked. Gypsy had a knack for scaring off big talk, too.

"What?" Cori said, gulping down water to clear her mouth.

"Gypsy," Danato scolded. "We don't know that will be the end result."

"Oh, I think we do," Gypsy offered him a smile when she said it, but her voice was cold.

"What is she talking about?" Cori leaned over to see Danato clearly past her. "Why would she think I would do that?"

Gypsy chuckled. "I love that panic in your eyes. You seem genuinely concerned."

Cori furrowed her brow at the sidelong accusation. "I am."

"No, you're concerned that you might be hurting someone with your actions. It is no more specific to me than it would be to a fuzzy rodent in a trap you put down."

"What?" Cori scanned the table for anyone to make sense of the words.

"Knock it off, Gypsy." Ethan gave her a glare that half demanded, half begged for her silence.

"It was just a question. I don't know why you are all getting bent out of shape about it."

"What the hell is she talking about?" Cori demanded.

"Gypsy was saved from a near-death experience the night Danato brought Ethan back," Belus answered before the topic could be blown off to protect the delicate woman. Cori looked over to her for confirmation, so she mimed her throat being slashed, starting with the high scar that was the start of the original deadly motion. Cori flushed and set down her fork.

Ethan gave Gypsy another scathing glare, and she resisted the urge to blow him a kiss. She was already irritating everyone to their maximum tolerances. She would need to hold back so they could calm down again.

"Her concern is that she will be put back in that same situation and not be saved by Danato, which would, of course, result in her death." Belus ended the statement bluntly, without any particular emotion. She respected his indifference to high-tempered situations. She wished she could be composed like that. Instead, she was struggling to keep from laughing at Cori's grief-stricken green face.

"Why didn't you tell me this?" Cori asked.

"Because they don't care," Gypsy said.

"That's not true." Danato lowered his voice and touched her hand. She glanced down at it, and he removed it. "Cori wished for you to be here as my employee. That being the case, you may have only been in that situation because of the wishes."

Cori nodded. "He's right, Gypsy. I don't remember seeing you that night. There was no altercation."

"You probably arrived too late, sweetheart. Do you remember seeing any dead bodies on your way through the alleys?" Gypsy expected her to wilt at the honesty of the question, but instead her eyes glazed and she searched her memory for corpsicles.

"The only other people I saw were a couple of men smoking in the alley. There weren't even any residents walking around."

Gypsy dug in, trying to make the hope drain from her face. "Maybe you missed it."

"No, I was trying to escape from Danato. I was looking at everything for a way out of the situation: stray cats, spewed garbage bags, fallen snow, and smokers. That's it. I never saw you. I never saw a body."

Cori seemed content with her evaluation. Whether what she was saying was true, didn't matter. She had convinced herself and everyone at the table that it was, so she was free to change the world back to what it was without guilt.

All the conversation proved to Gypsy was that Cori was willing to do whatever it took to get back to her old life.

Gypsy wondered how far *she* would go to keep her current life.

24

C ORI COULDN'T HELP BUT yawn as Danato and Belus examined her rings from either end of the couch. Gypsy was flopped over the arm of one of the easy chairs reading her magazine on the floor. Cori wasn't sure if the position was comfortable, or if she just liked to put herself in positions that drew attention to her.

Given the conversation at dinner, Cori was convinced that Gypsy was not only very messed up, but liked doing and saying things that made people dislike her. Rude, vulgar, or just plain weird was the only thing that Gypsy had to offer the social construct. She may well have been the ideal employee that Cori had wished for, but only because her disregard for others and herself allowed her to focus on her job. If that was what it took to get in Danato's good favor, Cori was glad to be the disfavored employee.

After she recovered from her yawn, she caught Ethan's eye. He was standing at the fireplace, watching her offer her hands to Danato and Belus for exploration. He smirked at her discomfort, and she smiled back. She felt a little less distant from him then.

"There seem to be markings on the rings, but they aren't very distinct," Belus said, using Danato's eyeglasses as a magnifying glass.

"Yeah," Cori said. "They're very Tolkien-ish."

Belus tried to remove the rings, despite what Cori had said about them being immobile. "That's amazing," he said to Danato. "It's like they are out of phase. I can feel them, but my fingers slip away when I try to pull."

Danato gave it a try as well. He made a valiant effort of strength, but the rings were set harder than the sword in the stone. "You've never been able to take them off?"

"I didn't, and then I couldn't," she answered. "What about you? You want a go at them?" Cori asked Ethan. His smile faded, and she thought the offer had annoyed him.

"No, I'll give it a try later," he said, winking suggestively and holding her gaze for a moment. She reminded herself that he wasn't hers, but it was getting harder to tell the difference.

"Why do you have elemental power stored in them?" Danato asked. "Don't tell me I actually allow you onto their level."

Cori laughed. "Not exactly, but I've had more than my share of run-ins with them lately. Hopefully, all that is behind me now." Cori pulled her hands away, and they both took the hint that she was done being manhandled. Danato moved to his chair and Belus shifted away from her.

Cori made it a point to yawn again. She wasn't sure she should just assume that a guest bedroom was available to her. Ethan smirked at her display and looked to Danato, who was already deep in a newspaper. "So, where did you plan to store her tonight?" he asked.

Danato grunted at the question before popping out of his newspaper. "Oh, sleep, yes, well..." Danato checked his watch. "It's a little early yet?"

"It's been a long day for me," Cori said.

Danato still didn't seem to understand. "Should I take her up?" Ethan asked. Danato looked him over suspiciously. "Unless you prefer to take her?"

"No, no, of course. Show her up." Danato ruffled his newspaper back into tension and buried himself in it.

"Come on," Ethan said as if it were a tiresome errand to show her the way. On her way out, she noticed that Gypsy had taken notice of their exit.

25

GYPSY WATCHED ETHAN SULK at the task of taking Cori upstairs, but she knew he was tickled to have another opportunity with her. Danato and Belus were oblivious to his interest in her. They assumed he was as content with his bachelor lifestyle as they were.

"Gypsy," Danato said, putting down his newspaper. "We need to talk about this."

"No, actually we don't," she said firmly.

"Yes, we do," he reasserted. "This situation has brought up a lot of questions. I'll be honest, I hadn't really thought about it affecting you."

"Why would you?" she asked.

Danato's head shook slightly, and he sighed. "Because I care about you," he said, as if that shouldn't be questioned, but it did need to be questioned. She wasn't exactly the lovable, kissable Cori, so why would he pretend that her existence mattered to him? "You've been with us for nearly three years. You are an excellent employee, and we would not want something bad to happen to you."

Gypsy smiled at him. It was fake, but she didn't see any point in bringing up the fact that he only mentioned her excellence as an employee. "I know, but you don't really think that I will live beyond that night."

"My hope is that you were just part of the wish. I hope that you won't ever be in that town. That's what I want to talk to you about. You have never shared your story with us—at least not the parts leading up to your... ordeal. Can you tell us now?"

Gypsy looked at Belus. He was content to lean against the arm of the couch and cross his arms. She wasn't sure she preferred to share her story with anyone, but somehow both of them at the same time seemed worse. She couldn't play on Belus's sympathies and she couldn't be so blunt with Danato. There was no game to be played. That wasn't fun at all.

"What does my past have to do with any of this?" she asked, sitting up in her chair.

"We want to know if there was a sudden change in your life that led you into your situation."

"I like how you use innocuous words to describe it, since 'captivity' wouldn't really specify which part of my life we are talking about."

Danato sighed in disgust and frustration.

"Cut the crap, Gypsy," Belus snarled. "We're doing this for you."

"Bullshit, you're doing it for your own peace of mind."

"No, we aren't," Belus continued. "What you don't seem to get is that all your anti-social defenses have achieved what you set out to do. We won't miss you."

"Belus," Danato tried to interject, but his objection stopped there.

"You usually respect my honesty, don't you?" Gypsy narrowed her eyes at him, but nodded. "Here it is. You shouldn't be here. Something changed to bring you here. Your whole life reeks of the intervention of a dark power. We just want to know when that intervention took place so that we can alleviate your fears. We couldn't care less otherwise."

Gypsy cleared her throat, if for no other reason than to break the silence following Belus's speech. "That was beautiful, Belus. I'm glad I can depend on you for honesty to the point of heartache."

"That's not exactly how I feel," Danato added, less enthusiastically.

"Oh, Danato, it doesn't matter. I was resigned to dying that night. You saving me just put me in a position that I didn't know what to do with, but made the best of. Belus is right. I am a complete nut job and a pain in the ass."

"Anti-social was the phrase I used," Belus corrected with a note of sourness for her paraphrasing.

"Yes, but what I'm trying to say is that I don't think *I* care."

"When did your life spin off course?" Danato asked, paying no heed to what was supposed to be her suicidal admission. All her best lines were lost on lesser minds.

"I don't know, really. I was out of college and working as a nurse." Gypsy paused, thinking about that part of her life again. It seemed like someone else's life. If they were right about the genie, it was *this* life that was someone else's. Cori's apparently. "I hated it. I had considered joining the military. I wanted to do... something different."

"You didn't though?" Danato asked.

"No, I chickened out. I stayed in my job, and got abducted when I took a vacation with my girlfriends."

"Had you joined the military, you wouldn't have been able to go on that vacation," Danato clarified, for her more than himself.

"Yes, that's right."

Danato nodded, pleased with that answer. "Good, that's a tremendous coincidence. That sounds like a designed skew in your life." He stood and left the room without another word.

Gypsy tipped her brow to Belus. "Well, I guess he's reassured. What about you, Ruthie?"

"You're just a bit more borderline than any of us wants to admit, aren't you?" he asked, tipping his head to examine her. "I don't think you understand what we're telling you. All that crap you went through with Mr. Throat-Slasher—the rapes, the beatings, the slave labor—you don't have to endure it, which means after this is all said and done, you will be free of all those bad memories, all the scars, emotional and physical. Gypsy, you can lead a normal life as a nurse, or a soldier, or whatever you want: family, kids, dog, and a white picket fence. That's even more than *we* hope for."

Gypsy let her mouth gape open. "Wow. That sounds like the tenth level of hell to me, and I've already seen the first nine."

Belus narrowed his eyes on her. He looked as if he had a scathing remark to brandish, but his enthusiasm for the rebuttal faded. He moved to the door offering no further commentary on her behavior, which was disappointing. He paused at the door before leaving, but didn't offer anything more.

As soon as the door shut, she rolled her eyes and leaned back in her chair with her magazine. "Who the fuck wants a dog when you can have a dragon?"

26

"So, are you and Gypsy... together?" Cori tried to ask the question casually, but Ethan no doubt suspected that she would be jealous of any relationship he had.

"You mean, are we shagging?" he said, touching the frame on the far wall of the spare room. He had been kind enough to show her in. Shutting the door behind him left room for his intentions to be known, but so far, he hadn't actually initiated anything.

"That's not exactly what I was saying, but yes, I guess that's the core of it."

"No, Gypsy doesn't do that," he said.

"Is she gay?" she asked.

"No, it's just..." He looked down at the bed as if he weren't sure he should sit with her on it. She wanted to be close to him, but she wasn't sure who he was. He seemed to be warming up to her, but she wasn't entirely sure he wasn't just trying harder to get her into bed. "Gypsy is her own kind of woman. She *flirts* a little with me, but she's never let me touch her. She had a bad time before she got here." Cori scooted back a little, offering more of the bed, and Ethan sat.

"Was she auctioned off like we were?" Cori asked.

"No, she was already a slave. She had finally had enough when we came upon her. On the way out of the village, we caught her having a heated discussion with some guy. Her owner, I guess. Danato barely had enough time to stop him."

"Stop him?" she asked. Ethan offered the throat-slashing motion less enthusiastically than Gypsy had. "Oh, right, that."

"She doesn't talk about it much, but Danato and I have learned to keep our distance from her. Too much attention, friendly or otherwise, tends to repel her, one of her many deep-rooted psychosexual circumventions. She works hard, but she's not the best socializer. So, no, we aren't a couple." He sighed as if the topic of Gypsy exasperated him. "Would that bother you?"

Cori paused, not sure how to answer that. "Definitely. I mean, you are my husband, after all." She chuckled to let him know she was joking, even though she wasn't.

"Technically, I *am* him, though."

Cori lost her amusement in the seriousness of his look. "I don't know. DNA sure, but personality, not so much."

"I am currently the only Ethan Pierce in existence. I have the same history, save the last two years."

"Are you trying to convince me or yourself?"

"I don't think you need convincing. You wouldn't have been bold enough to kiss me this morning if you didn't think I was the same Ethan."

Cori looked away. "I know you're Ethan, but you aren't *my* Ethan. You aren't the Ethan that loves me."

"You got to give me a little time to catch up, sweetness."

Her eyes snapped back to him, surprised by the familiar endearment. He smiled with flirtatious eyes that were also familiar. She smiled back, forgetting momentarily about the specifics of his identity. Their gaze held until reality bled over her desirous thoughts. "Why did you close that door?" She nodded to the closed door.

"For privacy."

She lost her smile. "Look, I won't lie. I love Ethan and nothing would make me happier in the middle of all this chaos than being in his arms, but it wouldn't be making love if I did it with you. It would just be a notch on your bedpost, and my ego won't allow that, no matter how satisfying it might be."

Ethan smirked at her. "Since you are being so honest, I won't lie either. Yes, I would love to do all that with you. Incidentally, I barely have enough notches to warrant a bedpost, but thank you for the confidence. However, the reason for the privacy wasn't so I could take your clothes off, it was so I could take your rings off."

Cori flushed with embarrassment before his entire statement set in. "Oh, I'm sorry, I just thought... wait, what? You can't take my rings off. No one can."

"Has Ethan tried?"

Cori furrowed her brow. She could remember telling him about the rings, but he never actually tried to get them off. "I don't think so, but why would it matter? No one else could."

"You've heard of the sword in the stone, right?" Ethan looped his finger under her hand and drew it to his lap.

"Yes," she said, watching him massage her skin.

"It's a little like that. Only in this case, the sword is a ring, and King Arthur is your husband."

"My husband isn't here," she purred, entranced by his tender touch.

"We'll see about that," he said as he twisted off one of the rings without difficulty. She gasped and scrambled to test the remaining rings again. They wouldn't budge.

"How did you do that?" She took the ring from him and slipped it back on. She tried to remove it again, but it wouldn't come off. "Do it again."

He wiggled the ring off easily. He removed a second and third as well. Cori laughed at seeing three naked fingers. "How?" She stared at him in awe. He smirked at her, letting the mystery drive her mad.

"Because I am your husband, after all."

27

"WHY WOULD EITHER OF you be able to remove the rings?" she said as he slipped off the last ring on her right hand. She touched the blanched skin where they had sat.

"Because," Ethan handed her the freed rings, and proceeded to her left hand, "the set was completed at your wedding."

"So?"

"So, I imagine your wedding vows contained something along the lines of love, honor, and blah, blah, blah."

"It was traditional, if that's what you mean."

"Mm-hmm, so you basically bound yourselves to each other." Ethan twisted the final ring that was her wedding band. She pulled her hand away before he could remove it entirely.

"Yes, we did." She looked down at the ring sheepishly. "I probably shouldn't remove all of them. Just in case they're allowing me to retain my memories of my old life."

"Sure." He held her eyes for a moment before standing. "I suspect that the writing on the rings is an apotropaic spell. The gold was most likely intended to repel or absorb harmful energy; to protect the wizard you took it from. Either way, they are doing both now. You are absorbing power and deflecting it when needed."

"How do you know this? Ethan never suspected anything when he gave them to me."

Ethan cleared his throat and took his usual militant stance. "I can harbor a guess. I assume that he stopped focusing on his studies after he passed the test."

"He..." Cori wanted to defend Ethan's devotions to his studies, but after thinking about it, she realized it had indeed been months since she had seen him with a book.

"I, on the other hand," Ethan continued without regard to her potential objection, "have remained focused on learning everything I can about all aspects of the preternatural world... which is easy to do when you don't have a wife or significant other." He said it flatly, but she could see he wasn't a happy bachelor.

She opened her mouth to offer thanks or appreciation for his knowledge, but somehow it seemed mocking. "I can see how the spell properties of the gold would have merged into a weaponized defense after being melted down." Cori set the removed rings on her bedside table and stood up. "But how were *you* able to remove them, when even I can't?"

He smiled and looked down. He drew her left hand up as if he might kiss it. "This ring is a symbol of Ethan's love for you." She nodded, even though she wasn't sure it was a question. "It's also a symbol of his ownership of you." Cori winced at the word *ownership*. He rolled his eyes at her. "Did you or did you not give yourself to him?"

"We gave ourselves to each other."

"Yes, but he's not wearing spellcast rings. You have to understand, spells are simply oaths. Whether they are written or verbal, if you mean them, and believe in them, they create their own power. The man who put this ring on your finger took claim of you that day. He promised to love, honor, and protect you until death do you part. In doing so, he bound you to him through the rings." Ethan caressed her wedding ring. "To answer your question, the reason I can take the rings off is because you belong to me."

Cori was aware of her mouth hanging open, offering no response to that statement. She wasn't entirely sure when they had closed the gap between them. Ethan took his time leaning toward her. She suspected he was waiting for her to object. Whether she should have—or even *could* have—was up for debate, but for the time being, her mind was reeling from what he had said.

Somewhere between realizing that she could finally get some answers about her rings and wondering what the hell *apotropaic* meant, his lips closed on hers. He wasn't as aggressive as before. The insistence that drove most men to get horizontal as soon as possible was on hold. His arm braced her back, pulling her paralyzed feet forward so their bodies could touch.

When she was certain that he wouldn't push her into something she wasn't yet sure about, she relaxed in his arms. He pulled away to look at her, before drawing her in for a deeper kiss. His free hand intertwined with hers and squeezed gently. In that moment, she wanted him. Not because he was different or the same, but because he was hers.

He drew himself away, releasing her back, hand, and lips simultaneously. He re-created the personal space he had infiltrated. She could see desire reflecting in his eyes, but he continued to back away toward the door. "Ethan—" She intended to offer him permission to proceed, but he cut her off before she could.

"I look forward to seeing you tomorrow. You should get some rest."

She wanted to ask him to stay, but she knew why he was pulling away. As difficult as it was for him to admit, he was scared of her. Scared of how much he enjoyed being with her. Cori had long since given up any doubts about Ethan's love for her, but she found it reassuring that even in this world, he was still drawn in by her.

28

C ORI KNEW IT WAS ridiculous to be running around the prison with Ethan and Gypsy. She should have been gone already. Just because she had 48 hours to spare didn't mean she needed to use them. She supposed part of her felt guilty about her mother. Another part of her was feeling guilty for Gypsy's circumstances. Despite Danato's assurances that Gypsy's life would be normal once the wishes were undone, she still felt like she was displacing her.

The chief reason she hadn't left, though, was because of Ethan. Last night's heated kiss aside, he seemed to have a working knowledge of her rings, or at least the craft that created it. She had more questions, and if he had answers or even just hypotheses, she wanted to hear them. Naturally, Gypsy and Ethan were called into work early to tend to a problem. The best way for Cori to get some time with him was to go along.

Third wheel didn't begin to describe how she felt running behind the Batman and Robin of the Kola Peninsula. She already knew that Gypsy was proficient with a sword, but Cori suspected she slept with her pistol under her pillow. Ethan outran them both and stopped just outside the seducers level.

When they caught up, Ethan glanced at Cori. "Maybe you should stay here."

"She wanted to come, Ethan," Gypsy scolded him. "If she can't handle this, then she shouldn't be taking my place." Gypsy checked the bullets in her cartridge before slamming it in and offering Ethan a childish tongue thrust.

"Have you ever dealt with Nikusui?" he asked Cori , blocking the door with his foot so Gypsy couldn't go ahead of him.

"No," Cori said sheepishly. "I know they're flesh-eaters."

"Nikusui are bitches from hell that can suck harder than a thirsty prostitute."

"Christ, Gypsy!" Ethan glared at her.

"I'm sorry, is this turning you on?" Gypsy asked with a well-performed fake sympathy in her voice.

Ethan opened the door for her. "Go!"

"Ladies first." She offered him the lead.

"Just stay back, and don't use your gun unless your life is in danger," Ethan said to Cori before he shoved Gypsy through the door ahead of him.

Cori looked down at the freshly assigned gun. It felt strange just being handed one, without any concern about whom she might shoot with it. She was a decent shot, but she was far more comfortable with her rings than the gun. She hoped that was a good thing.

Just outside the door, a young woman stood facing Ethan and Gypsy, eyeing them carefully. Cori's approach offered little interruption to her examination. She seemed to know who the threats were.

"Hey, Nuki. Whatcha doing outside your cage?" Gypsy drawled, sliding to the woman's right side. To Cori's confusion, Gypsy slipped her gun back into its holster and locked it down tightly. Ethan did the same and moved to the woman's left side.

Not sure what to do, Cori lowered her weapon, but didn't put it away. Ethan signaled her to stay, and she nodded. The woman before them resembled a reject from the cast of "The Grudge." Her long black hair was intentionally tied to drape over her face like beaded curtains. Her eyes split and looked at both Ethan and Gypsy as they approached.

Ethan attacked first and landed his face squarely on the woman's extended leg. Gypsy took her turn and ducked a fist, only to be met with the knee of the same leg that had hit Ethan.

Even with Ethan's lightning-fast return, his punch was blocked. Gypsy jumped back to her feet like a good martial arts student should and took a few punches as well. The Nuki may have looked human, but her movements were decidedly inhuman. She countered each punch and kick as if her two sides could work independently to defend themselves.

Cori took a few steps forward, drawn in by the teamwork that Ethan and Gypsy used. Ethan and she had spent so much time on separate paths lately. They never had a chance to work together like this.

After several lost blows, they started synchronizing their movements. Her left punch to his right was a mirror image. The duplicity must have confused the demon, because her defenses started to slip.

"You should have stayed where you belong, sucker-fish!" Gypsy chastised as they both got in a good kidney shot.

The Nuki bucked forward and her eyes shot forward, looking directly at Cori. Gypsy and Ethan noticed the change immediately and grabbed her arms to pull her down. The woman's mouth unhinged. The hissing sound she made sounded asthmatic, but the strong inhalation causing the noise didn't debilitate any of them.

Cori could feel a prickling sensation on her skin. When she looked down, she could see flakes of skin peeling from her body like the remnants of a bad sunburn. She felt the pain familiar only to those who have dared wax their legs. The pain radiated across her body, making her eyes water.

Ethan and Gypsy pulled their guns, but the woman pushed back against their restraining arms and threw them on either side of Cori.

She raised her own gun to shoot, but stopped when she felt a familiar pain. Her rings were burning. The hot glow of warded power dissipated the pain, and she no longer saw precarious levels of dandruff coming off her.

The Nuki tried harder, but to no avail. Finally, she released her maximum inhalation and stumbled from the effort without conclusion. Cori lifted her free hand and focused on the woman's body. She didn't want to kill her or hurt her, just offer enough of a blow to knock her off her guard.

The ball of fire wasn't large, but it shot out fast, hitting her in the chest. She flew back against the concrete wall behind her. The fireball had done little damage, but her head meeting the wall probably was more than necessary.

Ethan and Gypsy rushed over to collect the woman. Ethan took her torso while Gypsy held up her legs. "You okay?" Ethan asked as they carried her away.

"Yeah," Cori said, checking herself. She looked pink, but she wasn't in any pain. If anything, the experience had been like a full-body exfoliation.

When she looked back up to ask if they were okay, she caught sight of the glare Gypsy was offering her before they ducked into the back hall. Apparently, Gypsy didn't appreciate her help.

29

"HOW MAD IS SHE?" Cori asked when Ethan joined her in the cafeteria. He tossed her a bottle of aloe to soothe the pink of her skin.

"Don't worry about her," he said, slumping down in a chair across from her. He rubbed his forehead like he was coaxing away a headache.

"Are *you* mad?" she asked, wincing at the answer before he gave it.

"What's to be mad about?" he asked, lowering his hand to look at her.

"I tend to make a mess of things."

"What mess? The creature is imprisoned. No one got hurt. You got a free skin peel. It's a good day to me," he said, returning to his massaging.

"Still, I bet Gypsy ripped you a new one for letting me come along."

"I said don't worry about her," he snapped. Before Cori could decide how to feel about that, he reached over the table and touched her hand. "Gypsy's just Gypsy. I'm used to it, but it doesn't mean I want to relive it, or let it dominate our conversation. Okay?"

"Okay." She nodded and he let go so she could rub the aloe on her body. "Can I ask you a bunch of annoying questions now, or would you rather fetch an aspirin first?"

She could see his smile under his hands. She liked making him smile. It seemed to be a rare thing for him in this version of things. "Go ahead." He sounded exhausted, but the amusement in his voice told her he would rather be interrogated by her than reprimanded by Gypsy.

"How come the rings repel some powers and not others, and for that matter, why am I able to get shot while wearing them?"

"You've been shot?" he said, uncovering his eyes.

"Yeah. Never took, though, so it doesn't count." He narrowed his eyes at her and she smirked. "If I tell you everything, we'll never get back to my questions, and I really need to have answers."

"Cori, I'm not the ringkeeper. Honestly, last night was a lucky guess."

"An educated guess," she corrected, and he shrugged. "I need a few more educated guesses. Just help me understand what I'm missing. Fill in the gaps."

"Okay, tell me what you've absorbed and not absorbed." He sat up straight and leaned over the table for a proper conversation.

"I've absorbed the elemental powers, and Cleos's psychic power. I may or may not have absorbed some of the time bubble. I'm not really clear about how that particular nugget worked. I was trapped by a transmorph for several weeks without any major repercussions, and I got healed by a disperser without any interference by the rings."

"What's a disperser?"

"I only know of one, but you probably haven't met him. He's your best friend."

"I have a best friend?"

"Well, I can't qualify that. Heaton and Duke could be considered your best friends as well." He pinched his brow, no doubt surprised by at least one of those names. "Anyway," she said, touching his hand to draw his attention back to her. "About the rings?"

His attention turned to her hands instead of her questions. He drew her hand upward and slipped off a ring to examine it more closely. In the meantime, he kept her hand in his. "If the disperser wasn't hurting you, the rings wouldn't have blocked it."

"But why can't I disperse things then? Not that I've tried, but the only thing to ever come out of those rings has been tangible power."

"That's the answer then," he said, slipping the ring back on her finger. You likely have to touch the person to absorb the power, but more importantly, that power has to flow out of them and into your grasp.

"Nuki today was trying to hurt you. Once the rings established that, they blocked her power, but touching her would not transfer or initiate anything, so you could never absorb the power. So in that sense, yes, only tangible powers that are activated through the hands may be absorbed." She must have looked confused because he repositioned to explain further. "Your rings are the plug. The person with the power is the socket. You can't get power unless you touch the plug to the plug-in."

"Once I have the power, I seem to be charged indefinitely, but it's hard to make them work on command. Some powers come out better with some emotions. As you've seen, I tend to have accidents when I get overly agitated."

"The rings are designed to protect you. If you are in danger, your defenses rise. I can only assume that the emotions get earmarked during the absorption. If you want to keep wearing them, assuming Danato allows it, you will have to show him you can wield them as well as a gun."

Cori sputtered an objection that made him raise his brow. "Sorry, I probably should have mentioned that my gun privileges were revoked."

"Why was that?"

"I shot Belus." Cori said it so matter-of-factly that it surprised her when Ethan started laughing himself into tears.

"It's not funny, I almost killed him," she defended firmly, but she giggled at his uncontrollable reaction. "Speaking of guns," she spoke up to be heard over his riptide of guffaws. "Why can I be shot with them?" She leaned back to wait for an answer.

"That's easy," he said, bringing down his laughter to a finale of coughs. "Magic protects you from magic. Once you introduce manmade pain, you imbalance things. That's why there's no magic left in the world. The artificial energies cancel out the metaphysical ones, which by design are far weaker. That's why this place harbors so many piggy-backing creatures. Not a lot of technology, along with a high concentration of magical energy."

Cori smiled at him. She was starting to like this Ethan a lot. She wondered if her own Ethan might someday harbor the knowledge that he did. She was far from studious, and didn't have high hopes to know any more than she had to, but she could definitely see her Ethan someday knowing as much as Belus and Danato.

"Hey, what do you say we see what those things can do?" He smirked.

She intended to ask how Danato would feel about that, but she realized she didn't care. She wasn't really responsible for any repercussions in this version of reality, so there was no sense in getting excited about breaking a few rules.

30

G YPSY HAD LOST FACE. It wasn't about Cori specifically. She would have been pissed about anyone usurping her efforts. She had managed to restrain herself in front of Cori, but holding back that tide of emotions only left Ethan to take the brunt. She couldn't remember everything she said to him, but she definitely remembered slapping him. It wasn't the first time she had hit him, but this was the first time she thought he might actually hit her back.

That only added to her irritation. The game was being skewed by Cori's presence. She had long held Ethan under her boot heel, but he was getting bolder and cockier. She didn't understand how mere hours could change him so fast, but it was just one more reason for her to put a stop to this whole genie business before time was up.

31

C ORI'S YAWN PROMPTED A chuckle from Ethan. "How can you still be tired? You were asleep for nearly an hour."

"Yeah, thanks for that, by the way," she said, unable to contain another yawn. "I thought you said the rings would protect me from that?"

"They did." He snorted. "If they hadn't, you'd be asleep for a week."

"That's a pretty hefty risk for experimentation." She stopped midway through the section. The usual tweets, screeches, and chitters echoed around them. "I could get stuck here."

He stopped with a sigh. "A very high dose of adrenaline would have brought you out of it for long enough to make the request. I wasn't plotting against you." His voice was edged with disappointment at her accusation.

"Sorry," she mumbled and walked on with him.

"Since we are on that topic..." His feet slowed, but he didn't look at her as much as his own feet. "When were you planning on leaving?"

She smiled. "Trying to get rid of me already?"

"On the contrary." He stopped and met her gaze. "I just want to know how much longer I get to have you." Ethan offered no apologies for the subtext of the statement. Cori's lips and tongue felt too dry. She swallowed and remoistened before she could speak.

"I have time still."

"Why are you using it? You seemed so anxious to get back to... them." Cori wondered if he'd intended to say 'him.' She had stopped thinking of this Ethan as different to her own, especially since he was able to remove her rings, but she imagined that he still thought of this like an extramarital flirtation.

"I wanted to get some answers about my rings."

"Is that the only reason?" His eyes looked her over too quickly to be considered lecherous, but she'd have known what he was referring to with or without the hint.

"I'm enjoying myself, if that's what you're asking." He didn't seem to prefer that answer, but he nodded. "Are you?"

He smiled and narrowed his eyes. "Now, why does that seem like a loaded question?" He augmented his chest with his crossed arms.

"I was just curious. You didn't seem to care for me when you first met me."

"Oh," he drawled, as if he had uncovered her secret. "I hurt your feelings, didn't I?" She shrugged, not sure whether to acknowledge how much it had hurt her. "I wasn't sure how to take you, but rest assured, I am enjoying my time with you."

"Good," she said when nothing else occurred to her to say. "What's next?"

"Fred."

"Fred?"

"The monkey that rusts metal."

"Why would I want to rust metal?" she asked as they headed over to a plastic cage containing a spider monkey creature that chittered happily at their presence.

"It would help you get out of a jail cell. Just rust the lock and push."

"Yeah, that might come in handy," she said with a little more enthusiasm for the power. Ethan instructed her to pet the monkey. The eyes on the small primate head rolled back with enjoyment. "I didn't realize he was so domesticated."

"Yeah, he's very tame, but damn, does he cost us a lot of money when he gets out."

"Why do you guys have such a problem with that?" Cori asked. She could feel the rings warm as the animal's power filtered into them.

"What do you mean? Don't you have to fetch escaped prisoners?"

"Yes, but not very often. Ethan has trained his guards so well that they hardly ever make mistakes, and even when there is one, they rarely call us. They just handle it themselves."

"His guards?" Ethan leaned on the cage and gave a neck scratch to the monkey. The little guy leaned into it so much that he fell over.

"Yeah, Ethan essentially commands them now. Danato rarely instructs them." Ethan tried to appear uninterested in the statement, but she could see she was strumming his ego with her unintentional boast. "I guess the downside to that is we don't get to work together like you and Gypsy. You're a good team. I was a little jealous watching you two today."

Ethan stared at her, or through her. She wasn't sure what he was thinking, but it probably had little to do with what she just said, even if he heard it. "How often do you have escapes?"

"Well, not counting the elementals... maybe a dozen times a year, and usually that's just our escape artists on this level." She nodded to Fred, who was wiggling his leg at Ethan's next round of neck-scratching. "Why?" she asked when he didn't lose the glazed look in his eyes.

"Nothing." He snapped out of his trance and inhaled deeply, like he had been holding his breath. "Just curious."

Cori was about to ask about the sudden change in demeanor, but Belus's voice snapped her to attention. "What are you two doing?" She ripped her hands out of the cage so quickly she raked her knuckles. She contained the hiss of pain and turned to face him.

"I was showing her around, Belus," Ethan answered with a little more disregard than her Ethan ever would have used. "What do you want?"

"Danato wants to see her... and you, now," he said, turning on his heel and leaving without concern for their answer.

"Why does that always feel like I'm being called to the principal's office?" Cori asked. Ethan smiled and rested his hand on her back to usher her forward. She hoped that this meeting wouldn't take too long. She had limited time to experiment with her new powers before she had to go back. She hoped she could learn enough about the rings to educate Danato, so he wouldn't be so fearful of her wearing them.

32

I T WAS AMAZING TO Cori that even a decade after Belus's last cigarette, Danato's office still contained the stale smell of smoke. She wasn't sure why it also smelled like a garage, but somewhere between the mix of the two, the ticking clock, and the squeak of Danato's chair, it was home, even when she was about to get her ass ripped.

She slumped down in one of the chairs in front of the desk and sputtered the air through her lips. Ethan leaned against the wall instead of joining her. Belus took his usual spot atop the small file cabinet. Danato opened his mouth to speak, but her resonating *enthusiasm* baffled him. "What's wrong?"

"You tell me." She shrugged. "What did I do this time?"

"Do? Nothing. I just wanted to go over your test results with you. Why did you think you were in trouble?" Danato glanced at Belus.

"I only told them you wanted to talk to them," Belus said.

Cori turned and glared at him. "You might mention next time what it's for."

"I don't stipulate, I mandate," he said, losing some of his stone face to offer a slight glare.

Cori debated how far to take this. She knew she should let it go, but since Belus wasn't likely to start trusting her in this version of things, there was no harm in burning the bridge. "Listen up, you cold-blooded little toad." Danato's chair squeaked as she stood, but she didn't advance and neither did he. "It took me two years to earn the respect of Belus, and in those two years, he has earned my undivided loyalty and admiration as a mentor and a friend. I would not think twice about doing as *he* asks without question or complaint. You, however, are not *him*, and I am not wasting an ounce of what *he* has rightfully earned on you."

Belus's index finger tapped on the file cabinet. She assumed he was debating adding to that burning bridge. If he knew her better, he would have no trouble thinking of something to say that would put her back in her place, but without the familiarity, he had no hold on her.

Danato cleared his throat. "Okay Cori, you've made your point. Let's move on."

She sat back down and rubbed her forehead for a moment before turning her attention to Danato. He was watching Belus. Cori imagined she had pissed him off pretty good if Danato was monitoring him. Ethan kept his face forward like a good little soldier, but she could see the tinge of a smirk on his lips. "What did you want to show me?"

"I wanted to check with you on a couple of things. First off, your PET scan came back with an abnormality."

Cori cringed at the sound of that. The words *malignant* and *cancer* naturally popped into her head. Her mother and aunt had died of breast cancer, so she was careful to check for lumps, but brain cancer was so far off her radar she hadn't even considered it. "Tumor?" she asked, feeling the blood leave her face in preparation for hyperventilation.

"No, the PET scan didn't show anything like that. Psychics show a concentrated use of the pineal gland and prefrontal cortex and the primary visual cortex. It's the trifecta of psychic ability. To read someone else or predict the future, you need those three areas to be in sync and highly active." Cori tipped her brow. She didn't really care about anything after the *not a tumor* part. "Your scan shows low activity in pinpoint spots in each of those locations."

"What does that mean? I have brain damage?"

"I'm not sure. The areas aren't dead. They just aren't active, even when the areas are functioning normally for talking, reasoning, and moving. In all the images taken, the areas remain at even levels and in the same spots each time. The doctor said he wouldn't have noticed it since it is so small, except that it is consistent with each read. I guess I was hoping you might have an answer."

"So I'm anti-psychic?"

"Brain activity is highly subjective to the individual. Health and mental stresses can affect it dramatically. The reading is inconclusive, but it's something I wanted to bring to your attention. The dangers of working in an environment with psychic energies flying around isn't something to shrug off. As you well know, new problems are tripped over every day."

Cori nodded. She didn't have an answer for Danato, but she was certain if there were any problems with her brain, Cleos would be the first person to question. He had been in and out of her mind like a convenience store, so he was as much a suspect as a witness. "I'll look into that as soon as I get back."

"I take it you've come to terms with the outcome of returning your wishes?"

"You can't go home again." She shrugged. Going back to her old life may have been an option because the genie made it available, but the truth was, she wasn't the same person she had been at that time. She no longer wanted normal. She liked the abnormal, even if it was degrading her brain.

"Very true," Danato agreed.

"What was the second item you found?"

Danato glanced around the room as if he was unsure of how to break it to her. "Given the levels in your blood, I'm assuming I'm telling you something you already know, but..." Danato paused as if he were waiting for her to predict what he meant. "Cori, you're pregnant."

The blood drained back out of her face as she struggled to remember how to breathe. She shook her head, but there was no point in it. Danato wouldn't be wrong about that. The medical facilities at the prison were more than comparable to the outside world. In some areas, the technology exceeded it—the perks of private funding.

"I take it you didn't know?" he asked.

"No, we were discussing. Actually, Ethan was discussing. I was avoiding." Cori took in a deep breath. She hadn't felt sick or lethargic, but she knew it might be too early for that.

"You weren't trying, then."

"I must have miscalculated." She slumped down in her chair and tried to decide how to react. Was she happy? Was she sad? All she felt was shock and a resounding loneliness. She wanted her husband.

When she looked up at Ethan to at least see the face of the man she wanted, if not the actual man, he was half concerned and half pleased. Her Ethan, she imagined, would be trying to keep from bouncing off the walls with Danato right after. Since she still didn't know what to feel, it was nice to have a backboard of serene joy to balance her suppressed panic.

"Congratulations. I assume this will be a happy event?" Danato asked.

Cori took in a deep breath, and her voice pitched with faked enthusiasm. "Oh, of course. Ethan will be happy. You... the other you will be elated."

"I imagine so." Danato looked down, hiding his own pleasure at the idea of a baby. Cori wondered how she had ended up living with two men who were more baby-crazed than a woman. "It must be hard to hear this news from familiar strangers, but I thought you had a right to know."

"Yeah." Cori wasn't really agreeing or answering, just looking for words to fill in the space between his sentences.

33

I T WAS EASY TO forget about the expectations of the
real world once Cori came to the prison. It was clear
if she hadn't been kidnapped, she would have finished
school, got married, and had kids. It was the natural
progression of a relationship.

Cori looked at Ethan from across the field. She
knew he was cold, but she also knew he wouldn't
go inside until she came with him. He was patiently
waiting for her to clear her mind with fresh air. The
frigid air was leaving her incapable of thinking about
anything but her chattering teeth. So, in that sense, it
was working.

When it was clear she wasn't going inside, Ethan
made a slow approach to join her. Unprepared for
a long hiatus, his hands were stuffed into his pants
pockets so deep she wasn't entirely sure he hadn't poked
through the fabric to find warmth. He surveyed the area
as if he might find the tranquility required to withstand
the cold and enjoy the beauty of the landscape. Aside
from the endless grass patches that were tolerantly
awaiting spring, there was nothing of that magnitude.

"I don't know what I'm supposed to be feeling right now," Cori blurted out in case Ethan might have an answer.

"Supposed to?" He chuckled. "You can't 'supposed to' feel anything, you just feel it. There isn't a wrong answer."

"Oh, bullshit." Cori took in a deep breath to draw back in the intensity that was meant for another man. "I'm supposed to be happy and overjoyed at the thought of a baby. Any time babies are concerned, women are supposed to go weak in the knees."

Ethan smiled broadly, despite her obvious irritation. "Double whammy on the 'supposed to.' What do you *actually* feel?"

Cori rolled her eyes, but searched for the words. "Betrayed."

Ethan lost his smile at that particular description. "Can you explain that further?"

"I feel like I'm being pressured into doing this by Ethan and Danato. They don't even care what I want."

"Do you think Ethan has sabotaged your birth control methods?"

"No." She winced at the thought of depicting Ethan that way. "I just feel like a tool in this. A vessel. A host."

"Mmm." Ethan bit back his lips. "I won't bother highlighting the accuracy of that, but you do need to remember one thing. That baby is yours. Ethan has contributed his part, and you contributed yours. It's not some alien creature or eggs of a freakish insect; it's a human baby made by you and the one you love."

"Why am I the only one not happy? Even you're happy and you barely know me."

"That's true, but I'm a guy." Cori didn't need to ask what that meant; the expression on her face cued his explanation. "Guys don't think about the consequences or the long-term effects. They just think about two things: the pride in creating a new life, and a cute little kid to play with. You, on the other hand, are probably trying to figure out how to raise a child here." He motioned to their surroundings. "You're thinking about painful labor, diapers, and midnight feedings. You've probably even started to think about what your child's life will be like if he or she stays at this prison. Good, bad, or indifferent—you aren't sure if you want that same life for them."

"Why do you get this, and Ethan doesn't?"

"He's just in too deep. I've only begun to fall in love with you. I still have some rational thought on my side. He, on the other hand, can't stop thinking about a little girl with sloppy blond waves running to greet him when he comes home."

Cori ignored his comment about falling in love with her. She was feeling better about the situation. "What if it's a boy?"

"Well," he puffed up his chest, "I don't think I have to tell you how happy a man like Ethan would be to have a little version of himself to teach and train."

Cori smiled. "I guess if you just picture that image, it's not so scary."

"You just have to take it one step at a time. Don't leap before you know for sure a step won't do."

"Thank you," she took his hand in hers, "for everything." He glanced down at the familiarity, but did nothing to prevent it. "I know I'm unloading my emotional baggage on the wrong Ethan, but I really do appreciate the help."

He nodded and pulled his hand away. "No problem. Come on, let's get inside and test your rings." He offered her the lead, pressing his hand against her back as she passed.

34

Ethan brought Cori another cookie sheet, and she focused on the power she wanted to use. It surprised her that it took so much concentration to do what she usually did by accident, but she presumed it was the difference between pulling a trigger haphazardly and actually aiming to hit a target.

She'd honed the skill enough that she was able to sign her name in rust on the pan. She smiled and laughed at the ridiculous use of her newfound skill. When she looked up at Ethan, he was leaning on the opposite side of the island, watching her. The small smirk he had on his face made her forget what she was going to say.

"Danato's going to kill me when he finds out he has to buy new pans." Ethan broke his gaze and moved around beside her stool to view her artistry. "You still sign your name Reiger?" he said, touching the rust trail of her last name.

She shrugged. "I don't technically exist anymore, so the legality of a name change is rather pointless. It's not like I write a lot of checks either."

"Mmm." Ethan nodded in agreement. "I just got the impression that your Ethan was a little macho about his claims on you."

Cori giggled at listening to Ethan making judgments on himself. "I think his claims on me are more directed at my body than my signature."

Ethan nodded and took a long, lingering look over her body that made her shiver with the anticipation of possibilities. When his eyes met back with hers, he offered no apology or shyness for the libidinous examination. "I can see why," he said, not breaking the connection. Her mouth was desperately dry from hanging open, but she resisted licking her lips. "Do you want to move to the bedroom?" he asked, nodding toward the stairs.

Cori finally licked her lips and looked toward the stairs. "Umm," she stuttered, wondering how Ethan, in any version of reality, could reduce her to a puddle of desire, incapable of higher reasoning. "I thought... I wasn't sure that you...I mean, I do, but I don't know what Ethan would think."

Ethan chuckled softly. "I think if you are going to try out your sleeping skill, I should at least be in my own bed."

Cori blanched, embarrassed that she had once again misread his intentions. Part of her was also a little disappointed. "Oh, right, yeah, good idea." She stood up and whirled around, looking for something that she probably didn't lose, but couldn't help look for, anyway. When she realized she hadn't lost anything to begin with, she tossed her pan on the counter and headed upstairs. "Let's get this over with. I think I've trespassed on everyone's hospitality long enough."

35

AN HOUR LATER, CORI'S concern about overdosing Ethan was put to rest. She had tried nearly ten times to put him to sleep, and each time was incrementally longer, but it took a good deal of effort. The first time, she only got him to sleep for thirty seconds or so. The only advantage there was perhaps getting out of a really bad conversation. The last time she'd managed to get him to sleep for ten minutes, and this time she was up to 18 minutes. That was enough time to save herself if need be.

A passing thought occurred to her as she was watching Ethan sleep. She wondered if she could get away with using this on her child. Nap time would be a lot easier with this little power.

Ethan stirred. After he caught sight of her sitting on the edge of his bed with him, he smiled and stretched. "That felt like longer."

She nodded. "Almost twenty minutes."

"That's not bad. More useful than putting people to sleep for weeks at a time. You want to go again? This is the easiest work day I've ever had."

"No, I think I've learned about as much as I can here. I should probably go... see a lamp about a genie." She stood up, and he didn't move to intercept her, so she continued to the door.

"Are you sure?" he asked when she reached the door. "I mean, you still have time. Perhaps..." He let the statement stall out without any intention of finishing it.

She turned back to him and looked him over where he lay comfortably on the bed. She was impressed he wasn't taking advantage of the situation more, especially considering his unfettered advances from yesterday. He may have been a good deal shyer than his actions projected, especially with women that he knew more than a few hours.

"I do have time, but I don't think I have any more patience."

"What do you mean?" he asked before she had made her move clear.

She no longer cared whether this was her Ethan or not. The bottom line was, Ethan Xavier Pierce in *any* version of reality was hers, and there was no reason not to enjoy vicariously reliving her first time with him, through him.

She removed her t-shirt in one quick movement and kicked off her shoes. There was no point in making a strip tease out of jeans and a t-shirt, especially since he was already sitting up in preparation of talking her out of her decision.

"Cori, I don't think this is a good idea," he said, despite drinking in her bare skin.

She stepped out of her pants and straddled him on his bed. The house had not upgraded his bedroom to an apartment, but she was glad for the short distance between door and bed.

"Cori…"

She kissed him with as much passion as she had the other morning, but this time he didn't rush the moment. When he didn't make the next move, she lifted his shirt off and directed him to stand so she could remove his pants.

When he was fully unclothed, she was happy to see that his objections did not make it below his waistline. She didn't let herself quibble about the fine lines between making love, having sex, and a one-night stand. Instead, she kneeled down and drew him deep into her mouth, pleasuring him with copious enthusiasm.

He shuddered and let out a panting groan that made her ego bloom along with her desire. "Cori," he said breathily. "Please stop." He was clearly enjoying himself, so she didn't stop. When he gripped her shoulders and forced himself away from her, she looked up to see if she had misinterpreted everything she had felt from him.

He drew her to stand with shaking hands and caressed her cheek. "You are amazing, but if you don't let me stop you now, you won't get to feel me inside you." He slid his hand down into her underwear. "And I really don't want you to miss that." He slid his fingers inside of her.

"I had another appendage in mind," she said, touching his chest.

"So did I. I just wanted to make sure you were ready for me." His fingers were out of her and fumbling with her bra. His inexperience with the challenging garment left him fumbling around the front clasp. She was about to assist him when he ripped the brassiere open, freeing her breasts.

She yelped at the violent undertaking, but it quickly turned to a gasp when he reached between her legs and lifted her with his arm. Her thighs straddled his forearm, bringing her up to meet him. He freely suckled her breasts without so much as bending his head. She lamented through the raw assault on her nipples, but she pulled him closer, excited by the sheer animalism in his desire.

In her reality, Ethan had never been so unleashed in the bedroom, but she supposed that was her fault. Her past had hindered her comfort for aggression during sex. Yet now, in the throws with a man who didn't know to treat her prudently, she found no room for fear. Instead, her visceral hunger was demanding more.

She shifted against his arm to relieve her desperate search for more, but he shifted, dropping her onto the bed. "Not yet, sweetness," he whispered before tugging her panties off. She wondered if he would find it strange that he was using the same pet name for her in this life as in the other, but it wasn't a topic she wanted to bring up in the heat of things.

He crawled on top and pushed her hands down to the mattress. "No," she said instinctively, but didn't struggle against the restraint. She wrapped her legs around him and arched, begging for more. He pressed his body down on her and looked her over, either to keep control of his own rising hunger or simply to drive her mad with want. Either seemed just as possible.

Since she didn't have the strength to force him against her, she took a breather to focus on him as well. She looked over his familiar face and opened her mouth to say what came naturally to her in proximity to her husband. "I love you."

"What?" he asked, pulling one hand off of hers to brush her hair away from her face.

"I... love you," she said tentatively, when she realized she might have just freaked him out.

"You mean you love Ethan," he said, releasing her other hand so he could rest on his elbows over her. His lower body was still pressed against her, but she realized he wouldn't offer her any further pleasure if she didn't choose her words wisely.

"No, I love you. I will always love you. I don't care what ludicrous version of reality I end up in, you are still you. Maybe the memories are a little different, but your heart is still the same."

He looked her over somberly before kissing her gently. She expected he might jump off her and run away, but she felt him shift and push into her. For a moment, he pressed against her, letting her body accept his presence. He slipped his hands back over hers and began a slow, smooth, excruciating rhythm.

She pressed against him, demanding more, but he was refusing to offer it. She let him set the pace until she couldn't stand it any longer. She pulled her hands away from him and pushed him away. He reluctantly rolled off her, but welcomed her on top of him.

Once she had control, she pushed herself over the edge again and again. She was thankful that the house offered soundproofing since she wasn't being discreet with her culminations. When she was thoroughly exhausted, Ethan flipped her back over for one more finale that he joined her in.

36

"T HAT WAS INCREDIBLE," CORI said, dazed from the afterglow of cardio orgasms.

"Yes, it was." Ethan lay beside her, leaning his head on his hand and tracing his finger along her body. The delicate tickle of his finger gave her the chills, but she knew better than to disrupt his view with a blanket. "Better than with him?"

Cori smiled and turned to look at him. "Every time with *you* is incredible."

"Very diplomatic of you. Do you think he'll be mad about this?"

She shrugged. "I'm not sure, you tell me."

He stopped his hand over her belly like he might actually be able to sense the baby inside. It was the first time she had thought about being pregnant since she was told. She had thought about diapers, bottles, and baby-proofing, but this was the first time she thought about step one: growing the baby.

"I think he'll be angry at first. He won't like the idea of sharing you, but then he'll realize that I couldn't resist you any more than he could."

"As I recall, I started this."

"Yes, well, clearly he isn't doing his job if you couldn't make it 48 hours without my cock."

Cori chuckled. "In his defense, I was very busy, and then I was imprisoned, and then I was kidnapped, and then I made my last wish. Although the imprisonment didn't really stop us."

He looked at her dubiously, but decided that she wasn't kidding. "You lead a very raucous life, don't you?"

"I am a huge pain in the ass. Aside from sticking around for this," she trailed her finger along his bicep, "I really did need to get your input on these rings. I'm already in hot water for not revealing the whole truth about them, and now I'm going to have to tell him about the genie. I need to give Danato some answers upfront, so he doesn't panic and try to put me in a plastic bubble."

"He's that protective of you?"

Cori snorted derisively. "He's beyond protective, although lately I think he's been trying to ease up a little. Unfortunately, I'm not exactly helping that process by getting myself wrapped up in more drama."

Ethan nodded, more to acknowledge her words than to agree with them. "They'll take care of you, though, right? I mean, they won't... punish you."

Cori shook her head. "I imagine I'll need to do some pretty hefty negotiating with Danato, and some unpleasant groveling with Belus, or vice versa, but in the end, they'll just do their best to clean up my mess." He nodded again. "I should probably get cleaned up. I'd like to speak with Danato before I go back."

She started to get up, but he rolled on top of her. She thought he was intending to go for round two, but his panic-stricken face told her otherwise. "Don't go."

"What?"

"Stay with me."

"Ethan, what do you mean stay? I can't stay forever."

"The last person to ever tell me they loved me was my mother, and obviously you know how long ago that was. You can't leave me, not now. I think I'm in love with you. God help me, I've known you for a day, but I can't imagine being without you."

"Ethan, I'm not..." He kissed her ardently. When he pulled away, his eyes were brimming with tears. "Oh, Ethan, I'm not leaving you. I'm coming back to you."

"What if it doesn't work? What if you go back, but I'm just stuck here in this world?"

"I need you to trust me. I would never intentionally do anything to hurt you. If I go back, we can be together from the very start. You won't have to wait... well, not as long."

"We could make a life together here. You, me, and your mother." Cori cringed at his cruelty at including her mother in the negotiations. She pushed him off and started retrieving her clothes.

"We are both better off if things go back to the other way."

"Why?"

"Why?" she mirrored the question sarcastically. "Because of the relationship that I've built with Danato and Belus. I don't want to start from scratch again. Because of the relationships you've built with the guards, and with Daniel and Heaton. You are missing more than a few friends in this reality. Not to mention my accomplishments as a member of this team. If you think I had a raucous life there, imagine if I had to redo everything I've accomplished over the last few years. Some things just can't be redone. I have a right to my past, Ethan. I'm sorry if you think I'm being selfish, but I promise you, this is not your real life." She pulled on her underwear and jeans, giving up the idea of a shower in favor of a quick exit.

"Wait." He stopped her before she could piece together her bra and gripped her arms. "Okay, I get it. I didn't mean to insult the importance of your history, I just... want you. I'm not thinking about anything else."

"Ethan, you have to understand. You *are* him. I'm not leaving you. I'm just giving you back your memories. You have to trust me. Can you do that?"

He floundered for a moment before he nodded. "Okay, but I still want you to stay—for the night. You have until tomorrow night."

"I really shouldn't wait until the last minute to do this. That's how raucous starts."

"Tomorrow morning, for sure. Tonight: supper, maybe another round of bed wrestling, and then you fall asleep in my arms. Okay?"

Cori gave a perturbed sigh, but he had already talked her into staying longer.

37

"S O WHEN ARE YOU leaving?" Gypsy sat across from Cori, picking her teeth with a fork. Danato gave her a stern look, but turned to Cori for the answer as well.

"Tomorrow morning." Cori glanced at Ethan beside her. "Ethan has some interesting insights to my rings. He's very knowledgeable. He's helped me a lot."

"I bet he has." Gypsy flipped her fork around and licked the length of the handle suggestively. Though she meant it for Cori, Ethan's hard glare forced her attention to him. She smiled, pleased that her display was angering him.

Cori understood the intemperate rivalry that comes about when two people are partnered involuntarily, but with Gypsy and Ethan's relationship, there was no sexual tension, and as a working team, they were unparalleled. She didn't understand the pleasure Gypsy got from making Ethan mad, or anyone for that matter.

She decided Gypsy's social retardations were the last thing she wanted to get involved with, so she ignored the mock blow job she was giving her fork and searched for another topic of interest. "So, Belus, do you come here often?"

"What?" Belus looked up from his plate.

Cori heard a thwack and ping that also got Belus's attention. Gypsy's fork had taken up new residence on the floor near the door. Judging by Danato's murderous glare, it was clear that he was less than amused by her uncouth display. Cori pinched back her lips, refusing to take pleasure in anyone being chastised by Danato. Even though she found it hilarious.

When she looked back at Belus, he was waiting for her to repeat her question, or translate it. "Do you eat here often? Visit often?" she asked.

He shrugged. "I guess. Depends how busy I am. Why?" His question sounded defensive.

She sighed and leaned forward. "It's called small talk. I thought you'd be good at it." She winked at him, unable to resist the small joke. To her surprise, he didn't glare or offer a clever retort. He just stared at her, his brain still trying to wrap around her personality. She imagined that was how he always got under her skin so easily. He had observed her long before he'd ever reacted to her, which in and of itself, irritated the hell out of her.

"I don't mean to sound like I'm trying to get rid of you, but you really shouldn't wait too long," Danato said with unease in his voice. "Things tend to go awry very quickly here."

"Yes, I know, but there is one more subject that I wish to get Ethan's opinion on," Cori said.

"Well, go ahead." Danato nodded to Ethan. Cori glanced at him and he seemed to understand that the excuse of spending one more night together may not cut it with Danato.

"Speaking of things going awry," Ethan jumped in, saving her the trouble of a frantic mental search for a new topic of discussion. "Cori said we have an inordinate number of escapees at this facility."

"Well, I didn't say *inordinate*..." Cori clarified, seeing the mental volley that was happening between Danato, Ethan, and Gypsy.

"She says they only deal with escapes once a month or so."

"It depends on the activity in the prison," Cori amended, though no one was listening.

"What's your point, Ethan?" Gypsy asked.

"Yes, what *is* your point, Ethan?" Danato asked.

Ethan and Gypsy stared at each other for several seconds before Ethan finally looked away, finding new interest in his plate. "No point, just an observation. Something we should work on, I guess."

Danato looked between the two and then at Cori. She grimaced and shrugged. If there was something more to this argument, she was going to have to file it under things she didn't have time to deal with.

38

"I HEAR YOU'RE KNOCKED up," Gypsy added to her one-line conversation-starters after everyone had settled into the living room for coffee—and a touch of Irish for those wanting to partake. Cori noted that not only did Gypsy not partake, but no one even offered her the option.

"Crap, Gypsy, do you ever have an off switch?" Ethan sat down beside Cori on the couch. He placed his hand over the back of the sofa. She wasn't sure that had been his original destination, but that's where it ended up.

Gypsy waggled her head from her chair. "You can't even find the switch to turn me on. Why do think you'd be able to find the off?"

"Yes, I'm pregnant," Cori admitted, interrupting the banter. For once, she understood why Danato had thrown her and Ethan into the time bubble.

"I guess that's convenient. No confusion on the baby daddy front if you're already pregnant."

"Nope," Cori said flatly, not bothering to deny she was having sex with Ethan. She didn't want to get involved in this passive-aggressive Jerry Springer ruse for domination.

Cori was content knowing that she would never have to see Gypsy again after this was over, and that was enough to conciliate her temperament for rudeness.

"Aren't you afraid that fucking this Ethan will give your baby two heads or something?"

"Gypsy!" Danato scolded her from his chair, but he seemed more embarrassed by her than mad. It was Belus that was giving her a stare hard enough to crack glass.

"I don't imagine that would ever cross my mind," Cori said when Ethan's hands moved to his lap. He was fisting them, leaving half-circle tracks in his palms. "I'm sure once all this is over, things will go back to the way they were, without regard to any displeasing aberrations that arose because of my wishes." Cori couldn't resist one jab at her. Despite the mutual smiles between them, Gypsy didn't miss the intimation.

"I don't know, Cori. I think I would be worried about a lot of stuff if I were having a baby in this place. I mean, how do you begin to list those questions? Is my baby technically the property of Danato, since I am his slave?"

Cori felt an ache in her gut when she realized that did need to be answered—a question she had not thought of, and one she probably should have asked prior to getting pregnant.

"How will my child be educated?" Gypsy continued, twisting the knife in her gut with the rudest form of social interaction: the truth. "Who will my child play with, since there are no other children here? Does the child have to stay out of the prison, in which case, is this house their prison? Who watches the baby when I'm working or do I just automatically become a stay-at-home mom, which likewise makes me a prisoner of this house?"

"Gypsy, enough," Danato grumbled. "She isn't the first woman to contemplate having children in this facility. She'll get it figured out."

Cori was relieved to hear that she wasn't the first to consider all of this. "I have my concerns, Gypsy, but I will consult with my family on them rather than delve into 'what ifs' with you. You needn't worry, since you aren't the one having the baby."

"Well, not anymore," Gypsy whispered and winked at her.

Cori gave a quick scan around the room to see who had the answer to this particular ambiguity. Either no one heard it, or they were ignoring it to prevent further discussion on it. Cori jumped when Gypsy touched her hand with gentle intent. She was leaning across the corner of the coffee table. Ethan had leaned forward defensively, but the expression on Gypsy's face did not appear to precede violence.

For the first time, Cori saw Gypsy. She saw the real Gypsy, behind the tarantula eyes, perpetually lip-glossed smirk of condescending pride, and purple pigtails. If the warmth that was radiating off her was a mockery, it was her best performance yet.

"If it gets to be too much, Cori..." Gypsy whispered and squeezed her hand. Cori felt tears instantly spring to her eyes from an emotional memory she couldn't quite match with a visual one. "I know someone who can just make the baby go away."

It took a half second for Cori to realize what she meant by "go away," but before she could begin to be insulted by the suggestion of aborting her baby, Ethan was across her lap.

39

FOR A MOMENT, THE world went blank. Gypsy knew exactly what Ethan had done, but she wasn't entirely sure why. There was a scuffle and when she looked up, Danato had Ethan in a full nelson on the floor by the fireplace. Belus was towering over them, prepared to save Ethan from Danato if need be. Cori was still sitting on the couch debating on interfering or just bawling uselessly.

"What the fuck is wrong with you, Gypsy?" Ethan said, struggling almost hopelessly against Danato's hold.

Gypsy felt her cheek. He hadn't slapped her with his full strength, evident by her conscious state, but it was hard enough to seek out an ice pack and a painkiller.

She should have been delighted—she had finally won her game, but it was a hollow win. She had been working toward this moment for so long, keeping Danato and Ethan and even Belus on the brink of giving in to their baser instincts. She had predicted the day was coming soon, but she hadn't anticipated Ethan would be the first.

Despite Ethan's underdog triumph, Gypsy was not happy or proud of her accomplishment. Her game was based on the balancing act of anger and actual physical violence. Though the ultimate goal was always to break one of them, she'd wanted it to be on her terms.

Unfortunately, this time, she hadn't even been trying to make Ethan mad, let alone make him hit her. She didn't understand why her effort to counsel Cori on her options had finally defeated Ethan's chivalrous exterior.

"Nothing is wrong with me!" Gypsy defended on more than one level. "She has a right to choose." She looked at Cori, who had stopped crying as quickly as she'd started. "I just thought, given the difficult situation you have coming up, you'd want to know your options."

"You practically told her having a baby here is insane and she should abort it!" Ethan yelled. "What kind of person does that?" Gypsy tipped her head at Ethan. She didn't like this version of him. He was turning into Cori's Ethan right before her eyes.

"Gypsy's right," Cori said, making everyone turn to her. She looked at her with something resembling pity, but it was more emphatic. "I do deserve to have my options explained to me, even if I would never consider them." Cori touched her belly as if she were displaying her motherly instincts just by doing so. "Thank you."

Cori turned to the others and excused herself for the evening. She made the excuse of being tired, but she was clearly getting out of the way so everyone could yell at Gypsy. Danato and Ethan got up from the floor as if gentlemanly behavior still dictated they stand when a lady leaves the room.

"Aren't you going to apologize?" Ethan leered at her over the coffee table. She could tell he wanted to hit her again. Whatever this button was she had pushed, she wouldn't be able to un-push it.

"No. *You* hit *me*, remember? It's your turn to placate and pander."

"I meant to Cori."

Cori averted her eyes, trying to stay out of the argument altogether.

"I know what you meant."

He shook his head slowly, nostrils flaring. He looked like he was going to say more, but Cori touched his hand. The gentle gesture was enough to draw his gaze to her, and reduce the tenseness in his body.

It was fascinating to see how Cori sought to calm the men, while Gypsy loved nothing more than seeing their tempers flare. It was a sick hobby indeed, but she might have found a new game to play.

If Ethan was now out from under her thumb, there was only one final play to be made. Win or lose, it didn't matter anymore, since she would be dead either way.

C ORI DISENTANGLED HERSELF FROM Ethan's arms and slipped out of bed. He stirred slightly, hugging the pillow in her absence. She paused to enjoy the view of his Adonis body once more before she slipped out the door.

She tiptoed down the stairs, though she wasn't necessarily hiding her exit from anyone except Ethan. Sneaking away from him in the middle of the night wasn't a plan she was proud of, but she couldn't bear watching his face contort in grief when she had to say her final goodbye tomorrow... today. No amount of explanation would prevent him from thinking that she was abandoning him, so it was just best done quickly and with as little drama as possible.

She slipped out the front door and jogged over to the prison. Once inside, she headed straight for Danato's office to find the lamp. As agreed, the lamp sat on his desk to await her decision. It was strange to her that he would leave something so dangerous out in the open, but the lamp came with its own security measures. Plus, it wasn't like the prop room had ever been secure.

She picked up the lamp carefully by the handle and spout. Before she spoke the words, she went through a mental checklist, as anyone would before leaving for a long trip: keys, wallet, enchanted rings, and kneepads for upcoming groveling. There was one thing she forgot; something she wanted to do before she left. She couldn't do it when she got back—or at least it would be more difficult in her reality. She replaced the lamp and headed for the basement.

A cacophony of hoots, howls, and cage-rattling greeted Cori on the basement level. She slipped through the section divide and made her way to Cleos's cell. She hated seeing him behind bars instead of soundproof glass. She had firsthand knowledge of how much he detested the racquet of his neighboring photophobes, and unfortunately, her presence wasn't making things any quieter for him.

Cleos was curled up on his cot in a fetal position, with his ears covered. The creatures hounding her from the nearby cells were so loud that conversation was effectively off the table. She concentrated on her purpose and created a ball of flame that enveloped the corridor and scared back the monsters from their doors.

The majority of the noise ceased, and Cleos uncovered his ears. He looked up, baffled by the sudden silence accompanying her visit. His eyes looked dark from too much stress and not enough sleep. She couldn't remember if he'd even looked this run-down the first time she had met him.

"Cleos." She smiled and put her hands through the cage. "I don't have much time. I'm... leaving soon."

Cleos stood, but stayed just out of reach. He examined her with the same almost sexual gaze that he had mastered. "What exactly have you not much time for?" He tipped a brow at her, and she resisted smiling, since it would only encourage further flirtation.

"Cleos, I need... I want to talk to you."

He furrowed his brow. "I'm not accustomed to getting guests. Nor am I accustomed to entertaining them. I don't know what trickery you have planned for Danato, but you'll forgive me if I don't feel the need to participate in this." He turned around, making his proverbial, if not literal, exit.

"In my reality, I convinced Danato to put you in a glass cage so you didn't have to deal with the noise from your unruly neighbors." One such neighbor struggled in vain to get hold of her from the next cell. She zapped him with a spark that made him yelp and recoil into the darkness of his cage.

"Why would you do that?" Cleos asked, suddenly back at the bars, a good deal closer than he was before. Cori drew back a little, but kept her hands on the bars to let him know she wasn't afraid of him.

"It was a reward of sorts, for helping me take back the prison from the elementals when they escaped... the first time." Cleos chuckled and walked away again. "I know you don't believe I am who I say I am. Since you can't read me, I can't prove it, but I do have a question for you, one that you might be able to answer more honestly as a stranger than as my friend."

He linked his fingers in front of him and lifted his chin slightly, as if he were calling on her in a classroom. "Proceed, if you must, but be forewarned, I bore easily."

Cori nodded and shocked Cleos's grabby neighbor again—slow learner. "I've angered you."

"Not at all. Kill the little rodent if it pleases you," he retorted, misunderstanding her statement as a question.

"No, Cleos. In my version of things, these rings have been troublesome. I've done something to anger you."

"I don't anger easily." He shrugged.

"Yeah, but only because you're a cold revenge type of guy." Cori's smirk died before it was ever fully there. "I absorbed some of your powers and ignorantly used them... against you."

Cleos stepped forward, examining the rings a little closer. "*You* read *me*?"

"Yes." Cori swallowed hard. "I found out why you lobotomized those women."

"Erased, not lobotomized!" Cleos snapped, despite his claims against angering easily.

"Erased," she clarified.

"So, I am angry because you know the truth about my imprisonment?"

"You were displeased by the invasion because I delved into an area of your mind that is considered taboo, even for psychics. Apparently, what you do is overachieving, and what I did was... rude."

"Yes, I can see why you angered me."

"There was a good deal of argument, but you didn't get really angry until I forgave you for what you did." Cleos took in a deep breath, indicating that this reaction was not specific to their relationship. "My question is: why are you angry at me for forgiving you?"

Cleos looked around his cell like he hadn't bothered to look at it in the last decade. "Perhaps you're confused about what it is I'm mad about. Forgiveness implies you think I did something wrong. A soldier of war may feel guilty for killing his enemies, but for someone to forgive him for it would be insulting to his pride in duty."

"You aren't necessarily mad that I forgave you, but that I thought I needed to?"

"I assume if we are, as you say... *friends*," the word sounded foreign to his lips, "then I suppose that I would take even more insult to it."

"I'm still surprised you took it so badly. You've never claimed to be the good guy."

"Even bad guys have to draw a line somewhere. They don't often do it, but when they do, it's usually inflexible."

Cori sighed. "I don't suppose you have any advice for me?"

"You mean other than to stay away from me?"

"Many have tried and failed with that particular request. Once I establish friendship, you're kind of stuck with me."

"Interesting. Then perhaps you should know that I've never had a friend that I didn't use and abuse in some way. It's difficult to resist manipulating someone's mind when it's right at my fingertips. I doubt you would be the exception to that rule, regardless of our rapport."

Cori shook her head somberly. "You're one big act, Cleos. I know deep down that you aren't as heartless as you pretend to be."

"And how do you know that?" He double-dog-dared her to answer.

"Because," she tapped the metal bars, "you're in this cage." Cori walked away before he could respond.

He was definitely Cleos, but, like Ethan, he was a version that her presence hadn't impacted. She pushed open the airlock to the last section before the elevators.

If she gained nothing else from this messed up version of "It's a Wonderful Life," she would at least now know that... walking into a section full of *escaped* photophobes was a fantastically bad idea.

"Oh, shit." Cori stared down the line of snarling, drooling, mostly vampiric creatures that were wandering the corridor section between her and the elevators. They stared back at her, elated by the happy accident. She wasn't quite as pleased by it, but she was definitely electrified.

41

GYPSY HAD A PLAN. It wasn't complex or well thought out, but it was artfully diabolic and she was very proud of it.

As with most achievements worth bragging about, she started from scratch. In this case, that meant starting with the bottom-dwellers. When she caught Cori in the basement talking to one of the photophobes, she thought her plan might be thwarted before it had started. But Gypsy was nothing if not resilient. A few unlocked doors later, and she was on her way back up the stairs.

She skipped through the main foyer to Danato's office and removed her gun before entering. She eyed the lamp on his desk warily at first, but then abruptly picked it up by the spout and flipped it up in the air. She barely caught it by the handle and stuffed it into a drawstring bag before securing it to her belt.

She turned around to leave, but found Belus standing in the door to the office. His hard glower said a thousand things, and none of them were nice. She couldn't help but smile at this little curve ball. He was always so intuitive, which meant it was harder to manipulate him. For once, she didn't even have to try. The truth was out in the open, and it was ugly.

"I knew you would try something like this," he said, still maintaining a casual lean on the doorframe, even though they both knew he was just staying close to her gun.

"You did? I didn't. I just came up with it."

"You're just a walking time bomb."

Gypsy clicked her tongue and waved her index finger at him. "No, no, Ruthie, the phrase is *bombshell*." She winked at him, but the humor disappeared into the abyss of tension between them.

"You're a sociopath, Gypsy."

"Isn't that just a big scientific word for asshole?" She rubbed her tongue across the exposed teeth in her smile.

"I don't think you were meant to be this way. I think you just can't balance out the good and bad memories. I think you would have been better off dying in that alley."

Gypsy finally lost her cocky smirk. It wasn't a shock to hear him say it, but the sympathy in his tone surprised her. He honestly thought death was the only way to fix her irreverent cynicism for life. "You could fix that, or at least try." She glanced at the spot where her gun was on the other side of the wall.

"You think you can pull that sword before I can get this gun?" His eyes motioned to the sword hanging awkwardly on her left hip. She could pull it and stab him in one graceful movement, but whether she would be fast enough to avoid a gunshot wound was another thing altogether.

"If I'm going to die, I'd rather it be by you. At least I know you wouldn't sob over me while I take my last breaths."

"Even if I did, they wouldn't be for you," he said.

She perked an eyebrow at the strange statement, but didn't pursue an explanation. "Let's get this over with so I can get back to freeing the prisoners."

Belus's eyes widened, and he reached for the gun without a pre-emptive catch phrase. He trusted that he could reach the gun before she could even pull her sword, so he didn't duck for cover behind the wall. He was right about the sword, of course, but he didn't take into account the blade she had concealed near the small of her back.

She drew it and whipped it at his chest. The knife buried in just to the right of his sternum. There may have been residual brain activity, but for all intents and purposes, he was dead the second the knife sliced through his heart.

He didn't fall to the floor so much as crumple, but the result was still the same. He was face up on the white linoleum in an expanding pool of blood. Gypsy considered pulling the knife out to reuse it, but she thought it looked better right where it was.

She retrieved her gun, which wasn't far from Belus's hand. He had been so close. It was a good try, but alas, she was just too good.

42

C ORI SLAMMED AGAINST THE bars with the help of eight anemic bodies. She was disappointed to find that her electrified response was of little consequence against their bloodlust. She managed to shock several hands and faces at once, but the overwhelming numbers only resulted in a rearrangement of the immediate threat.

One set of teeth latched onto her wrist. Another latched on at her collarbone. She screamed, but the exertion was pointless when there was no one around to help. She had wisely snuck out of the house so her absence would be less traumatizing. Now Ethan would find her dead instead of just gone.

She pushed away three other faces that were trying to nuzzle into her flesh like nursing puppies. Puppies with very sharp teeth. She could feel the energy drain out of her, along with her blood. She had to do something.

She focused her thoughts on anger, and revenge, and anything else that would draw on her fickle ring power. She felt her hand ice over and the slobbery beast attached to her wrist pulled away from her distasteful coldness. With both hands free, she pushed her neck-sucker free and headbutted him. It wasn't generally a move in her repertoire since her head wasn't quite as protected as Ethan's, but she knew vampires had notoriously fragile bones.

The creature was an easy knockout and his collapse left her room to kick and punch a few more away so she could activate her fire power. After two more singed creatures retreated to lick their wounds, she started the process all over again with the remaining five.

Vampires may not have been strong, but in packs, they were as tenacious as werewolves.

43

O N THE WAY BACK through to the stairs, Gypsy paused and looked toward the gym. She smirked and ran over to make a quick amendment to her plan. She pulled the lever to the hangar doors and impatiently waited for them to open.

The dragon slept blissfully within until Gypsy fired half her clip at her. The scales protected the creature from being riddled with bullet holes, but that didn't mean it didn't sting like a son of a bitch.

"Wakey, wakey," she taunted. The creature moaned in complaint, but barely moved. Gypsy knew she had pissed her off, and in twenty or thirty minutes, someone was going to find out just how much. Oh, boy howdy, were they going to find out!

Gypsy headed back to the stairs to her next destination. She saved the animal level for later. She skipped the part-time level since there weren't any werewolves available during this moon phase—oh, what a beautiful mess that would have made. She also skipped the transmorphs because she wanted to know exactly who was who. Not to mention, she was an original, and damn if she was going to share this glory with anyone. She took the seducers level carte blanche, just to supplement the chaos. Most of the seducers had to remain locked up, since they were just as dangerous to her as everyone else.

She stepped into the room that held the time bubble. The massive half orb shimmered, the precursor to Efrat's independent exit. The bubble expelled him, allowing him the dignity of stepping away with barely a falter. He used a tuning fork he pulled from his back pocket to recover from his deafness. He slowly realized he wasn't alone and stilled, prepared to defend himself.

Despite his preparation for battle, she only paused briefly to acknowledge his arrival. "Efrat," she said cordially as she passed him on her way to the lookout booth.

"Gypsy," he countered with the same *what the hell* expression he always gave her when they met. She had discovered him on more than one occasion roaming free in the prison, but since she didn't exactly want to draw attention to her own after-hours visits, she had never mentioned it to Danato. Naturally, he didn't trust that she wouldn't tattle about his comings and goings, so he remained leery of her. At some point she did plan to capture him in exchange for a little suck-up slack with Danato, but as of thirty minutes ago, she was well beyond ass-kissing.

She climbed the Navy-style stairs to the booth. Efrat had already knocked the man designated to watch the bubble out, conveniently saving her time and a bullet. She looked over the system control panel, which was a veritable blur of screens, dials, and something-o-meters. The only thing remotely interpretable was the classic big red button. It was under locked glass, and as she understood it, was *NEVER* to be pushed.

"What are you doing?" Efrat called up to her.

Gypsy slammed the glass with her elbow, which resulted in a new bruise, but no breakage. "I'm pulling the plug."

His eyes widened, and he looked at the bubble beside him. "You're letting the wizards out?"

"God, no! Well, inadvertently perhaps. I'm just clamping the bitch's feeding tube." Gypsy hit the glass with the butt of her gun.

"Why would you do that?"

Gypsy paused and leaned on the control panel to search for the right words. She scratched her temple with the barrel of her gun, which probably said more about her state of mind than her words could. "You know that tiny little thread of hope you have that keeps you from going certifiably insane? The one that lets you believe that maybe someday you'll get out of this prison alive?"

"Yeah," he agreed cautiously.

"Mine broke." She batted her eyes at him and laughed at the disbelief on his face before going back to access her big red button of doom.

"Well, mine is still intact, so I can't let you do this."

Gypsy chuckled again. She could feel the room alight with static, but it was too late for all that. "I like you, Efrat," she said, looking down at him. The admission stalled his attack as she'd thought it would. "There's something alleviating about knowing you'll hurt me every time you touch me." His confusion dimmed, and his usual self-pity-inspired irritation returned. "We really should have hit a movie or something."

She cut the crap out of her fingers, trying to weasel them through the glass, but when she reached pay dirt, a massive bleating alarm started. While Efrat was trying to figure out what was happening, she unloaded a few shots into the panel to keep anyone from undoing her mayhem.

"Are you crazy?" Efrat yelled as she holstered her gun on her thigh and slid down the ladder, leaving a trail of blood from her cut hand.

"Probably, but I think we've established that." She crossed her arms and leaned back to offer her ultimatum. "Now, Efrat, you have two choices. You can try to escape while all holy hell is erupting. Or you can use those magic hands of yours to feed this bitch, so she doesn't start seeking out exterior sources of food. The choice is yours."

She could tell he wanted to barbeque her with one shot, but something inside of him was still trying to be the hero. His cape had been ripped off and his pockets were filled with kryptonite, but he was still trying to fly. It was admirable, pointless, but still worthy of respect.

Gypsy stepped forward and kissed Efrat. He threw open his hands to avoid touching her, but he didn't back away from the kiss. When she pulled away from him, his head was consciously or otherwise negating an unspoken question. "You are a fucking nut job."

"Awe, you say the sweetest things. Better get to work, hero."

He glared at her but focused his electricity onto the time bubble, to keep the entity that maintained it happily fed.

44

C ORI STUMBLED OUT OF the elevator covered in scratches, bites, and the dreg from the basement floor. She didn't even want to begin thinking about what diseases she might contract as a result of it. She simply committed herself to getting back to her own world so she could sterilize her skin.

The short trip to Danato's office was even shorter since she ran the last few meters. "Belus!" Cori slid into base beside Belus, smearing her pants with blood. She checked for a pulse, but he was long gone. She stared down at her dead mentor for the second time in her life and cried.

She suddenly snapped out of her reverie when she remembered the lamp. She could undo it all. There was no reason Belus had to die. She could save him… again.

The lamp was gone. She looked around, searching the drawers of the desk, just to be sure, but it was gone.

The puzzle pieces of this disaster were only beginning to fall together when Danato and Ethan arrived. Ethan had his gun in hand and was prepared to shoot whoever had killed Belus. Cori raised her bloody hands defensively.

"I know what this looks like, but I didn't kill him," Cori stammered and wiped her hands on her shirt.

"I know you didn't." Danato stared down at Belus. Ethan lowered his gun as soon as Danato acknowledged it. "That's Gypsy's knife." He and Ethan exchanged a look. Ethan ran off to find and apprehend her, but the rage on his face hinted at the condition she would be in when he returned with her.

Danato raised his eyes back to her. "Are you okay?"

"Yes. I went to see Cleos again before I left. The photophobes were out. I may have injured a few of them rather severely, but I don't think I killed any." He gave her a slight smile. "And the lamp is gone."

His eyes bugged out, and he scanned the room, searching for it. "She's trying to stop you from leaving. Belus must have gotten in her way."

"He underestimated how determined she was." Cori couldn't help but stare at the knife in Belus's chest.

"We all did. I need to—" Danato silenced when the office juddered as if it was sitting on a miniature fault line. Cori steadied herself against the desk. Danato seemed unaffected by the tremor outside of the door. The color drained from his face, and the rarest emotion seeped into his eyes—fear. "Oh, Christ, she unplugged her."

Danato disappeared down the hall. Cori had several questions about the event, but no time to get answers. Instead, she added them to her mental list of *things Danato won't talk about*. She didn't understand what was going on, but she assumed it was an extension of her life's goal to attract pandemonium. Indirectly or otherwise, she had made a mess of things and she needed to undo it. She needed to get the lamp back by any means necessary.

On her way out the door, she paused over Belus's body and let the image burn into her mind. She wondered if this might be the second occasion that she would have to willingly kill someone. Her rings offered a good defense and offense, but she wasn't sure she had the proficiency to compete with Gypsy's acrobatic strength.

She reached down and pulled the knife out of Belus's chest. The jagged edge caught on his rib cage and she gagged, unable to be indifferent to the body she was pulling it from.

She heard the elevator *ponk* down the hall and she sprinted to catch up. "Danato!" She jumped the railing to skip the short steps just as he entered the lift. "Danato, wait, I can help."

Cori reached the open doors just in time to see the elevator phase out of existence, along with Danato. She reached for him, but her hand hit a wall that shouldn't have been there. "Danato?" She hammered on the cinder blocks with her fists, but there was no response from within. She felt the chipped, faded yellow paint on the wall. The elevator was gone, or perhaps had never really been there.

More questions that needed to be answered, but not now.

She changed her approach to the stairs, but another thrumming vibration in the floor halted her. The rumble accompanying it culminated in the adjoining wall to the gym ripping open. Penelope bulldozed through the wall into the foyer space that was barely large enough for her. She roared furiously at the world and all who inhabited it.

Unfortunately, Cori was the only one around to take the punishment for whatever she was mad about.

45

GYPSY UNLEASHED THE CHROMANDI and watched them intermittently run, sniff, and run down the corridor. At first glance, they appeared human, but they were worse than dogs. At least you could train a dog to be useful. The only thing the Chromandi did consistently was eat, and they didn't particularly understand the distinction between fresh meat and living meat.

"Gypsy." Ethan's voice was low with threat, or perhaps it was a promise. Either way, it made her breathe in the moment. She could smell him: un-bathed sex, lingering cologne, and that little something that made him a man. "Look at me!" His voice resonated through the high ceiling rafters.

She turned at her leisure to face him. He was still several meters away, but she knew he could make the distance in two muscular leaps. She expected to see anger on his face, but that was the least of his emotions. The disillusionment suffused with anguish deserved to be photographed and framed.

The nonverbal exchange between them was poised and reverent, but it was still a call to war for both of them. Any other man would have already been a minute into a tirade, but not Ethan. He was deathly still. He hadn't even raised his gun to aim at her. It was planted against his hip, ready in a heartbeat.

"You should have bludgeoned me from behind," she said, stepping sideways to make him flinch.

"Why?" He contrasted her movement, and they began to circle. This was going to be an epic fight. She couldn't wait to find out who was going to win.

"Why what... specifically?"

"Why *everything*, Gypsy?" Ethan enunciated. "Or perhaps I should ask how? How can you kill one of your own? How can you destroy everything? How can you do this... to me?"

"My answer to all of the above is... why not?"

"I thought we were at least partners. We were never going to be lovers. We weren't exactly friends, but we had each other's back."

"And now you have Cori's back. And front."

"What pisses you off more, Gypsy? That she loves me, or that she's capable of love?"

Gypsy bit her lip until she tasted blood. "You think I'm not capable of love?"

"I think you're capable of coveting, but not love."

"Is there a difference?" She perked her brow in amusement. But he didn't share in it.

"If you loved me, you would not make me kill you."

"If *you* loved *me*, you would understand that I can't do that." She narrowed her eyes, waiting for his response, which took some time.

"I don't understand anything about you. Why have you been letting the prisoners out?"

"Oh, figured that out, did you? Well, we had to do something, didn't we? I mean fuck, this place is boring when it's running efficiently."

"Gypsy, please—"

"Don't beg! Groveling is the most detestable form of negotiating. I've done plenty of begging, praying, and bartering in my life, and believe me, none of it works. This is ending tonight, Ethan, and if you want things to go back to normal, then you're going to need this." Gypsy tapped the drawstring bag hanging from her belt.

Ethan focused on the bag, no doubt thinking of all the ways that he could take it from her. "Why not just let her go back? Why not rewrite your own life so you don't have to be scarred by it?"

"I don't *want* a new life, Ethan. I'm pretty fucking fond of the one I got. You're going to have to pry this from my corpse if you want it." Gypsy could see the battle raging in Ethan's eyes, but when he finally made up his mind, there was no turning back.

46

CORI GRUNTED UNDER PENELOPE'S paw, wondering how she had ever managed to make it through her final test with a male dragon. She pushed as hard as she could on the pads that were pressing down on her, but it was useless.

Penelope was happily asleep, but Cori wasn't sure for how long. She was just impressed that the big beast was susceptible to the sleeping touch.

Cori pried her toes apart and squirmed from underneath the massive weight. When she was finally out, she leaned against her foot to catch her breath before heading upstairs. There was a melee of guards going up and down the stairwell. She heard screams several flights up and decided that the second floor was a good place to start her search.

Bruised and bloody, she stepped out near the infirmary. She could see through the glass walls that the nurses were aiding several guards in the waiting area. By the looks of things, they were treating bites, and severe ones at that. There were too damn many biters in this prison.

She ran toward the next section. Several steps from the door, she tripped and fell. She looked behind her and caught a glimpse of a cat-sized creature scurrying away. She jumped up and took an inventory of herself and surroundings. She appeared to be intact, and there was no sign of an ambush by tiny creatures, so she moved on to the next section.

47

C ORI ENTERED THE SECTION just as the fight between Ethan and Gypsy began. It was difficult to say who'd ignited the fuse. They both just lunged at each other full force. It was easy to assume that a gun battle would go to the fastest draw, but despite being armed, neither drew their guns.

Gypsy ducked low, just missing Ethan's fist. She slid on her knee-high socks, upper-cutting his crotch as she passed.

He kneed her in the chin. She grabbed his leg and pushed him, forcing him off balance.

She stood, but Ethan was already on top of her. Gypsy backflipped away from him. She landed on all fours in a runner's crouch. She drove forward.

He used her momentum to throw her several yards away. She landed hard on her hip, which left her limping back to the fight.

Cori couldn't help but be impressed by her vigor. There weren't many men that would dare take Ethan on. A woman capable of not getting her face smashed in had more than luck on her side. Gypsy and Ethan had trained for this moment for years.

Gypsy drew her sword and slashed at Ethan's chest. He jumped back, barely keeping his shirt intact. She chopped down toward his shoulder with no notable intent to stop at the last second.

Ethan twisted out of her way and punched the flat side of the sword. The metal blade snapped and the upper half clanged against the floor. Gypsy withdrew and Ethan advanced.

Ethan grabbed her by the shoulders and drew her back in preparation for a head butt.

"Ethan!" Cori yelled, but it was too late.

Gypsy pulled her gun and shot him in the stomach. For a moment, he just stood there with her. The unspoken rule regarding guns had been broken. As dire as the situation already was, Ethan must have assumed that Gypsy would still fight fair.

Ethan stumbled back and Gypsy turned her gun on Cori. Before Cori could think *electromagnetic deflection*, she pulled the trigger. The gun snapped quietly, impotently.

Cori and Gypsy exchanged looks before the firefight began on Cori's end. Motivated by her conflicting emotions, she barraged the woman with fire and lightning. Gypsy couldn't begin to out run it. Instead, she dove behind a steel-walled cage.

Cori heard the smack of Gypsy's cartridge being loaded. She rounded the corner with fire already ablaze, so she didn't lose the upper hand. Gypsy punched her in the stomach from her stooped position.

Cori tumbled to the floor and Gypsy grabbed her hair, yanking her back upright again. She shoved the barrel of her gun into Cori's temple.

Cori gripped her wrists, trying to get control of her body as well as the situation. "Uh-uh-uh, no flame, no bolts, or I shoot." She twisted them both to face Ethan. He was sprawled on the floor, bleeding prodigiously, but he was still alive. "Ethan!"

"Gypsy, please," he pleaded.

"Shut up," Gypsy yelled and coughed. She pulled Cori's head back to put the gun under her chin. "I want you to watch her—" Gypsy coughed again, and spat liquid from her mouth. "I want... you..." Gypsy struggled to breathe.

Cori tightened her grip on Gypsy's wrists and pried the gun away from her face. She focused all her thoughts on how much this woman disgusted her and how much she wanted her dead so she could go home.

Gypsy's eyes widened when her exhales only resulted in convulsing up water. Cori wasn't the maniacal type, but she couldn't help but smile at the obscure water power coming out to give Gypsy a proper sendoff.

She thought it would be hard to watch someone die, but when it was someone as fucked up as Gypsy Grace, she didn't feel the least bit sorry for ridding the world of her existence. Whatever she was or could have been didn't matter now. Something had flipped her switch from good to evil long ago, and Cori had no intention of suffering for it.

Gypsy seemed to understand what was happening and just let go. She looked at Cori, examining the woman who had killed her. She was no doubt disappointed that she was beat out by Cori's endless dumb luck.

Up close, Cori could see the determination in her eyes. She might have been dying, but damn if she was going to cry or show fear. It was strangely familiar. It reminded Cori of Nevia's cold, dutiful, apathy, but with Gypsy it was hot, self-serving antipathy.

They were strange attributes for... a nurse.

48

ORI'S MIND RIPPLED AS the singular memory coalesced. She pulled away from Gypsy, unable to finish her task now that she remembered where and when she had met her.

"Grace!" Cori announced while Gypsy coughed up water. "Grace Gypsum!" Gypsy was still grappling for air, but looked at her curiously when she said her real name. "You were one of the nurses at Memorial Sloan in New York. My mother, Emily, was a patient there... for a time."

"A lot of people were in that cancer ward. Why would I remember her?" Gypsy croaked.

"Because you watched her die." Gypsy looked at her through hooded eyes. "You quit that same night. In this reality, she didn't die, though. You didn't quit; you ended up in the wrong place just in time for my wish to be granted. Don't you see, Gypsy? Your whole life changed because of me, but I can change it back. You don't have to be this damaged person."

"Why is everyone trying to change me? I'm not gay, I'm not Catholic. I'm just a bitch. There's nothing you can do to change that."

"I can take away the pain!"

"The pain is all I have!" Gypsy stood wielding her gun, but not quite aiming it yet. "I don't remember anything before the pain. That life is gone. This place is all I have of good tangible memories, and you want to take it away!"

Cori took a step back. Her hands pulsed with electricity, not entirely by choice. "I want to help you, so you can have your whole life."

"You're a hypocrite. You don't want to give this place up either."

"That's different."

"Why?"

"I belong here; you don't. I hate to play the first come, first served card, but this is an aberration. You aren't supposed to be here."

"Something you should know about me. I don't follow the rules." Gypsy raised the gun and fired.

49

I T WASN'T OBVIOUS TO Cori that she had been shot. At least not right away. The searing pain was a good indication, but she couldn't actually differentiate where the pain was coming from. She assumed that was a good sign, but the longer she lay there staring at the ceiling, struggling to find oxygen, the more she knew it wasn't.

Gypsy eventually came into view above her. Her pistol sagged by her side, still wafting smoke. Cori waited for her to lift the barrel to her lips and blow it off, but she didn't. She just stared down at her with a vacant expression, radiating indifference.

Cori opened her mouth to say something scolding and derisive, but blood spilled from her mouth instead of words. She touched her throat and found it wet. She confirmed it was blood, despite that being an obvious conclusion. She wasn't gushing, but she presumed that most of it was dripping back into her lungs—thus her difficulty breathing.

There is a moment between new enemies when a quick assessment is made. For robust opponents, the evaluation reveals who is stronger? For smart opponents, who is keener? In this particular case, there was no assessment to be made. Gypsy had already won, and they both knew it.

Cori continued to gape at her, waiting for her to bestow a final witticism from her ample pink lips. Instead, she straddled her, sitting on her stomach—as if breathing wasn't hard enough. Cori reflexively coughed, but she forced herself to stop, since it was only going to escalate her suffering.

Cori grabbed Gypsy's legs and tried to push her off, to get some relief, but she didn't have the strength. Gypsy's legs frosted where she touched them, but it wasn't enough to hurt her. Cori's unnatural defenses were wavering, either because she was weak or focused too much on her pain.

She coughed abruptly and for some reason still felt compelled to twist to one side so she didn't get blood on Gypsy. The knife she had taken from Belus's chest pressed into her back. She reached for it.

With no hope of survival, it was only revenge that prompted her to pull it from her waistband. She thrust it into Gypsy before she even recognized the threat. The frosted blade sunk into her chest, not far from where she had taken it from Belus's.

Gypsy stared down at the foreign object. She was confused by its sudden appearance and no doubt surprised by the quick turn of the table. She huffed a stuttered laugh that sounded more like weeping, but Cori knew better

than to mistake it for real sentiment. Gypsy's eyes dulled
and she slumped over.

50

"**C**ORI!" ETHAN SMACKED HER face, but she barely felt it. She opened her eyes and saw Ethan overtop her. For a moment, she thought it was over and she was back where she belonged, but the pain in her neck and the blood spilling from Ethan's abdomen told her otherwise. "I've got to get you to the infirmary."

He lifted her, but he groaned and released her. Cori coughed, struggling to filter air through the torrent of blood draining into her lungs. She didn't have much time, and judging by the lack of color in Ethan's face, neither did he.

She reached for the bag on Gypsy's belt. It didn't readily break away, but Ethan leaned over and tugged it. He winced, but it separated. He brought it to her. "What if it doesn't work?"

She touched his cheek and attempted to tell him to trust her, but it was barely intelligible. She drew the lamp out of the bag and held it by the spout and handle. "Ge-ee," she coughed.

A thick cloud of white smoke billowed from the lamp and formed into the genie. He towered over her, muscled, tattooed, and vaguely translucent. He looked over the situation as if he were disappointed by what he saw.

"I…" She swallowed the blood currently in her way. "espet…ho…oafa." She enunciated as careful as she could through the blood.

The genie's disappointment dampened further as he slowly shook his head. She raised the lamp to him and pointed at her wound, and rolled her hand. She wanted to get on with the magic while she was still able to breathe.

"Genie!" Ethan yelled. "Send her back. Un-grant her wishes."

"I must hear the words precisely." His jaw set and he looked almost angry.

Ethan grabbed the lamp from her and held it in his face. "She accepts your offer."

"It must be her words," he said.

"She's drowning in her own blood. She can't say them any clearer. You know what she wants. You know what she means."

"The laws are defined," the genie said, staring only at Cori.

"She is *dying*!" Ethan winced from the pain of yelling.

Cori grappled for the lamp again and tried to speak the words more clearly, but this time the blood was even preventing her from breathing, let alone speaking. She coughed up blood and got an idea. She used the blood to write the words on the floor. Pleased with the blood transcript, she looked up hopefully to the genie.

He kneeled down before her, pressing his knee into the words. "The only way that would work is if you knew cuneiform."

Cori reached for his hand, but he drew it back and shook his head. She offered an explanation by grabbing her own hand and guiding it to write on the floor. She looked at him hopefully, but he shook his head again.

"*You* are not permitted to touch *me*, and my helping you would be severely punished."

Cori could feel the onset of dizziness and she realized she wouldn't make it much longer. She again dipped her finger into the blood that might have been hers or Ethan's or Gypsy's and traced a word above her previous request.

Please!

She looked at the genie, pleading her case with every ounce of her heart. He was the closest being to a god she would ever meet. There was no way that he didn't have the capacity and power to bend the rules.

"You have no comprehension of what you are asking." His eyes narrowed, and she could tell that it was not just an insult to ask him to bend the rules, but dangerous.

Ethan collapsed beside her, face first, into the floor. His lips were now purple, and she couldn't see if his chest was expanding.

Cori tapped the floor under the *please* repeatedly. She didn't have the luxury of being concerned for the trials the genie would have to endure for helping her. She had to save herself, and thereby everyone around her.

This version of reality was beyond hope, and she would rather die now than stay without her friends, but if there was even a microscopic chance to change it all back, she was not opposed to groveling for it.

"I have never broken a rule this important," the genie explained, but she could see his demeanor turning to dread, like he was already contemplating doing it. "What you ask today is a grave debt, one which you cannot repay. I will sacrifice for you, but know that it is not a demonstration of my mercy to do so. I will require a sacrifice in return." Cori nodded. She already owed the genie three sacrifices for negating her wishes; what was one more minor inconvenience? "I will collect my debt when our contract is complete."

She nodded. There was no time to argue or ask questions. She could no longer feel her limbs and she was almost positive that the stars surrounding the genie's head were not from him.

"I will not be able to remove the wounds. You will not be out of danger."

She nodded again. That was the last thing she was worried about. She may have hated going to the prison infirmary for minor injuries, but just short of miraculous intervention, they would do anything to save her. She did, however, wonder if her blood loss was going to affect her pregnancy.

The world blurred around her, either because of magical transformation, or because she was passing out. Either way, she was in someone else's hands now.

51

D ANATO SCOFFED. HE COULDN'T believe how ridiculously anarchic the last few days had been. The prison was practically under siege with aberrations. He was exploiting his prisoners to capture his renters. Cori had joined the ranks of the elementals. Belus was going to take yet another rebellious, loud-mouthed, cocksure asshole under his wing. The one remotely level-headed employee he had left in his midst had apparently just instigated the sparks that could start a civil war between the werewolves and the Council of the Moon.

And all of it could be traced back to one tiny little mistake.

"Is that it?" he asked, looking over the faces before him. "Does anyone have any more life-altering news? Cori has supernatural powers. My least favorite prisoner—who, by the way, I am not getting paid to house anymore—is going to be mentored by Belus. My best hunting team is probably going to become the most *hunted* team. A boatload of military men have to be deep wiped and shipped back to the U.S. Not to mention eight fucking months of paperwork to explain this to my superiors!"

Danato stood up and leaned over the desk to look at Cori. "All of this because of one fucking key!"

Cori shrank before him, and tears sprouted in her eyes. She had made a lot of mistakes in her time at the prison, but this one had compounded with so many more mistakes. He loved her more than he ever thought possible, but he didn't know how else to get through to her.

Despite what Belus believed, she hadn't been any more translucent with him. If she couldn't trust him, Belus, or even Ethan, then he wasn't sure there was going to be a place for her in this prison. He didn't want to be the one to demote her, but he also didn't want to slough off the responsibility to Belus just to save face with Cori. He had brought her to the prison to begin with. He was going to have to be the one to take her out of it.

"I'm sorry I doubted you, Danato." Cori's voice cracked. "I really am. I just wish things could just go back to normal."

"Oh, son of a bitch," Efrat mumbled from behind Cori. "Tell me you didn't just say that."

Danato looked back at Efrat. "What's your problem?"

Before Efrat could answer, the space around Cori blurred. The glossy orb surrounding her rippled and exploded, throwing everyone in the room back. When Danato found his bearings, he saw Cori slumped over in her chair, covered in blood.

"Cori!" Ethan yelled and crawled to her aid. Danato was barely aware that Belus was on the phone calling the infirmary for an emergency blood transfusion. Ethan picked up his wife and carried her to the door that Efrat was holding open for him.

"Tell Daniel we need him," Belus said, already on his second phone call. "Infirmary, now!" The phone receiver clanked down and Danato turned to him.

"What the hell just happened here?" he asked, still dazed.

Belus didn't shrug, but the blank stare he offered told him he didn't know any more than he did.

"She made a wish," Efrat said, still standing in the doorway. Danato hadn't even realized he was still there.

"So, what?" Danato narrowed his eyes at him.

Efrat shook his head. "She kept forgetting. It was bound to happen, eventually."

"What was bound to happen?" Danato yelled.

"When Cori was jumping around in time, trying to talk me into saving Belus. She bumped into a genie's lamp."

Danato's mouth fell open, and a laugh came out. It was far from funny, but he had reached his limit on yelling. He couldn't believe there was yet another detail that he didn't know about.

"Bastard was pretty persistent, but she didn't exactly have time to deal with him, so she just refused to make any wishes."

Danato looked at Belus, and he found the same worried expression on his face. "Unbelievable," Belus murmured.

"What did she just wish for?" Danato asked out loud, but he was mostly talking to himself. "To go back to normal?" He looked around. "But nothing has changed."

"How would we know if it had?" Belus pointed out.

"Why would she be injured?" Danato glanced at Efrat, hoping that he might have more hidden insight, but he didn't offer any.

"Knowing Cori, something went wrong," Belus said.

"Maybe she wished her way back," Efrat suggested. "With a hole in her neck," he added, mocking his own stupidity for the idea.

"You don't think she made a deal?" Danato asked Belus.

Belus nodded. "Knowing Cori..." He trailed off, and they both headed to the door.

52

BELUS LEFT WITHOUT ANOTHER thought to Efrat. Danato stopped at the door and looked at him squarely. "You're seeing this, right?" Efrat perked his brow, confused. "You see me running around fixing the mistakes of others, trying to hold the walls of this prison together, by sheer will and luck."

Efrat nodded. "What's your point?"

Danato slammed the door shut, and Efrat backed away from his advance. He put his hands behind his back and shook his head, refusing to be provoked.

"The only reason I haven't signed your execution order is because I'm in the middle of a whole lot of shit right now. If you want to hide behind Belus and be his guinea pig good deed for the year, then you'd better start your ass-kissing before I get done with all this. Because the only thing I'm going to remember about tonight is that you almost cut my girl's hands off. So, if you try to hurt my people again, I will execute you myself." Danato moved back to the door.

"I thought that was Belus's job." Efrat's words froze Danato's withdrawal. "Or did I read that file wrong?"

Danato turned back and saw the mild smile on Efrat's face. He walked back to him slowly, rested his cane against the desk, and put his face directly in his. To his credit, Efrat kept his hands behind his back. It was probably the only thing that was preventing Danato from literally smashing his skull between his hands.

"Give me one reason," Danato whispered and clamped Efrat's arms behind his back. "Give me one reason why I shouldn't rip your arms off, and remember, that's not an exaggeration when I say it."

Efrat struggled fruitlessly under his strength. Danato couldn't deny the enjoyment he got from seeing a man realize that he had no chance of overpowering him. He had never been as reserved as Ethan, but his years with his cane had made him less grandiose in his displays.

Efrat's bravado waned and Danato drew his arms out, careful to keep his hands out of reach and aim. "Okay, Danato, you've proved your point," Efrat groaned.

"Apparently I haven't, or you would have already given me a reason."

"Cori, she's the reason. She wants to save me."

"I doubt she'd miss your arms after you tried to cut her hands off." Danato kept his voice low and calm.

"I was stupid." Efrat gasped as one of his shoulders popped out of socket.

"Clearly, but what's your reason? You've delved into my personal files. You must know how far I'll go to protect my prison, so give me a reason not to rip these weapons off you. Show me a sign that you can be trusted, or at least not despised."

"I'm ashamed!" Efrat howled in pain. "Cori… I finally made her hate me. I hurt her deeply, and I'm more ashamed of that than anything else I've done here." Danato relaxed the tension on his partial quartering.

"Cori went against you and Belus and her own husband to save me, and I threw that sacrifice back in her face like it was trash. I need to do something to make up for that." Danato released him and took a step back while Efrat struggled to roll his shoulders back into alignment.

"You want a reason to keep me alive, then use me as a scapegoat. I manipulated her. I made her believe that you were hiding something. I took advantage of that part of her that wants to believe that everyone is good. I am to blame for everything, Danato, starting with that damn key."

"That's very noble of you, but I think we are beyond saving Cori from demotion."

"What if it wasn't her?" Efrat said, stepping after him.

"What?"

"Look, I'm not sure what effects those rings have on her mind, but once in a while, she sort of slips back into Dr. Frank's memories. You saw it tonight."

"She's done that before?" Danato cringed at yet another problem that would have to be sorted out.

"Yeah, maybe a couple more. I think it's like a record getting stuck. She just needs a whack to get back on the right track. Whatever she absorbed from Jillian wasn't just memories. She must have absorbed her thoughts and feelings, too."

"That would be a Cleos specialty," Danato mumbled. "I suppose we could try that as an excuse. Make it sound like she was not of sound mind."

Efrat took in a deep breath, like he was content with the help he had offered. Danato looked him over. "You aren't completely off the hook, you know?"

"I don't mind the hook. I just don't want to be in a frying pan."

Danato offered what might have been a smile if it had stuck around longer. "And also... if you ever mention that file to me or anyone else again, it won't be the frying pan. It'll be the fire."

Efrat stiffened and raised his chin obediently in soldier formation. "Yes, sir," he grumbled.

53

T HE ROOM WAS DIM, and the sunlight coming through the tall window by the sink only served to highlight the dust in the air, but it was the same kitchen that she had arrived in when she'd finished making her third wish. Cori danced around looking for her mother, but she was alone. The smell of leather and liquor replaced the vague smell of blueberry scones.

Cori checked her body for the last wound. She sensed pain, but it radiated distantly from everywhere, as if even her mind didn't know where it was coming from. Her outfit was back to the same old t-shirt and jeans. It was a far cry from her high heels and jumper, but at least she was back to some part of normal... or rather abnormal.

She had wished for normal, but she was only beginning to realize that she didn't really want that. If there was any way to bring her mother back without hurting anyone and without changing the course of history, she would do it in a second. She certainly wouldn't mind giving up two weeks of memorable beatings and molestations, but it was a part of her now. She couldn't undo death and dire circumstances *and* still hope to be where she wanted to be, which was with Ethan and Danato and Belus.

"He took a good deal of that pain away, you know," Cleos said as he entered the kitchen and propped himself against a counter. He was swirling around a brown liquor that, for some reason, she knew was scotch. Too many lessons with Belus, she supposed.

"Are you going to slip into my unconscious every time I pass out?" she asked, crossing her arms and leaning back in much the same way.

"Sometime I'll have to fill you in on the details of my amusement regarding that statement. To sum up the basics again, you are turning up on *my* doorstep. It's like walking into someone else's house and accusing them of trespassing. I am intrigued that you managed to change my construct, though." He looked around the room. "You must be very preoccupied with this place."

Cori nodded, but didn't bother asking about the latter statements. It was far too late in the game to start asking questions that didn't pertain to the plot at hand. Like everything in her life, there was a time for questions, and there was a time to let her enigmatic men remain dedicated to their selective mutism.

"Your memories of those two weeks," Cleos continued with regard to his arriving comment. "The incidents in the wandering village—he blurred them a bit. It makes them easier to ignore. Not that you wouldn't have gotten there on your own, but he felt obligated to do so, since you didn't know enough to ask."

"I wouldn't have asked," she said dismissively.

"That's why he never mentioned it." He cocked his head smugly.

"Deception is in the details," Cori said, with more venom than she intended. "Am I back in my real life?"

"Yes," Cleos said. "I think you'll be disappointed to find that the same protection that the rings offered your memory has also allowed you to retain your battle wounds."

Cori rolled her eyes. "I should have just killed her right away," she mumbled.

"Well, now, that wouldn't be *you*, though, would it?" Cleos pulled himself from the counter and approached her. "Poor Cori, you trust the bad guys far too often."

"You aren't a bad guy. Stop trying to convince me that you are."

"Oh, come on. Tell me you weren't just a little sickened by my entourage of flawed personalities."

"I think you're a finagling businessman, but I don't think you are bad."

"Is there a difference?" He winked and walked over to the tufted leather fainting couch that had no business being in the middle of her mother's kitchen. He sat down and crossed his legs. Cori could hear the distant din of his party, but nothing else had changed.

"Why don't I remember being here when I wake up?"

"Because, Corinthia, this memory is not housed in your mind—it's even pretty deep in Cleos's mind. This part of you"—he pointed to her—"and this part of him"—he pointed to himself—"are the only ones who know. It's very complicated, and I do look forward to seeing how angry Cleos will get when he finally discovers what you've done."

"He's already angry with me."

"Then you'd better send flowers and chocolates, cause your dog house is about to get a second story."

"I spoke to the other you, from the wish reality. He said Cleos was mad because I forgave him for something he was proud of. Is that true? Is he proud of what he did to those women?"

"Aren't you? Isn't that why you forgave him? To offer approval of what he did?"

"No. I mean, I think he did what he thought was best."

"So, if it was for the best, then why forgive him for it? When someone does something well, we thank them, or congratulate them. We don't forgive soldiers for killing in war. We throw parades for them."

"It's such a simple misunderstanding, though. Why did he react so... strongly?"

"Cleos doesn't have a long list of good deeds. He also doesn't have a long list of good friends. For one of those good friends to belittle his good deeds... it sort of takes a chunk out of his lists."

"How can I make him forgive me?"

"Now, why would I help you do that?" Cleos simpered mischievously.

"Because you know that I love him," she said flatly.

He nodded, impassive at the statement. "Eventually, you might break him, but be patient. Cleos is not easily swayed to give up his convictions. His pride is what keeps him imprisoned, not his crimes." Cleos tilted his head, listening to something. "Oh, I think I hear your ride coming."

54

ORI SAT UP IN bed and took a deep breath. She pawed at her neck to feel for blood, but there was nothing there, not even a bandage. A slight bubble in the tissue was all that was left of her bullet wound.

"Daniel took care of it." Nevia startled her. She was sitting on a metal chair some distance from her bed. She expected to see a magazine or a book in her hand, but she was without distraction. She wasn't sure if that meant she hadn't been there long, or she had been there too long.

"What...?" Cori's voice croaked and Nevia jumped up to pour her a glass of water from her bedside table.

"The voice will heal in time. Daniel isn't that proficient yet."

Cori guzzled the water and noticed the IV in the crook of her elbow. She looked over at the blood transfusion she was being given. Between blood suckers and a gunshot wound, she must have lost a lot of blood. "How long was I out?"

Nevia looked at her watch to give her a more exact measure of time. "Eighteen hours. You've been out since you got the injury. They worked on you for nearly an hour to stabilize you before they would let Daniel in to help. Danato and Ethan had to take turns keeping him out." A small smile passed over her lips, but it was gone as soon as it came. "After he healed you, he passed out." Cori suddenly realized that Nevia was not conversing with her so much as reporting to get her up to speed.

"He woke again around six this morning and left with Heaton on the truck at seven. I took over watch for Ethan at about that same time, so he could sleep. In case it matters, I had to badger him for over a half hour to get him to leave."

Cori smiled at Nevia's consideration. She was pleased that she was here to help, but wondered why she hadn't left with her team.

"Danato's been in about every hour on the hour to check on you. Belus slipped in a couple of times to speak with the nurses."

Cori couldn't help but snort. Belus would use any opportunity he could to do that. Nevia raised her eyebrow, but Cori just shook her head. "How long have you been here, then?" Nevia looked at her watch again. "Approximately," Cori added.

"Six hours. It's a little past one... tomorrow to you," she added, since Cori had missed out on the passing night to remind her what day they were on.

"Wow." She was impressed by Nevia's fortitude and tolerance for boredom. "I thought we were still on a get-well card sort of basis, but I appreciate your dedication."

"I had a few ulterior reasons for coming, but you're welcome."

"You wanted to avoid going back on the same truck with Daniel, didn't you?" Nevia's mouth thinned. "I'm not sure what all the background is, but from what I gathered in the office, you two are on the rocks."

Nevia shrugged. "We are just two very different people."

Cori could hear the disappointment in her voice. It was the conviction of someone frustrated with a bad relationship and wanted to get out of it. It was also sadness that the relationship was not working despite the desire to keep it. She had heard it many times in her own voice.

"In this business, I imagine there aren't a lot of people to choose from. Signing disclosure agreements probably isn't the best icebreaker." Cori chuckled, but Nevia didn't join in. "Did Daniel ever tell you about our first meeting?" Nevia shook her head. "I was in much the same condition I am now, in a hospital bed. I woke expecting to see Danato or Ethan, but instead I got him." Nevia gave her a small smile, hinting that she understood her disappointment.

"He had come to check me out. See if I was good enough for his friend—a friend who, by the way, he had barely just met." Cori took a drink from her glass again to moisten her throat. "He assessed, in our short meeting, that no, I was not worthy, because no one was. I had an instant hate for him because of that. It's taken a while to get over it."

"Were you just conversing, or was that a metaphor for me?"

"Mmm." Cori held up a finger as she finished another swallow of water. "My point is, Daniel is an ass upon first meeting." Nevia laughed. Cori assumed she hadn't told her anything she didn't already know. "However, I think he's a genuinely good man."

Nevia sobered and nodded. "I agree, but I think we might have rushed into a physical relationship before we were ready for an emotional one."

Cori laughed this time. "No one is ready for an emotional relationship, least of all Daniel."

"Actually, I think Daniel is ready for it. It's *me* who is having doubts."

Cori furrowed her brow. "Is that because of the fem-wolves?"

"Partially, but I think it's more about what I want from a man."

"What do you want?" Cori asked.

"I want a man I can be proud of." Nevia looked down at her feet. "I know Daniel is good, and he has such an amazing power, but he acts like a child. How could he be a husband or a father?" Cori's brow rose, hearing how far Nevia had planned her life. "I mean, I could never introduce him to my parents. He's too crass. Just because he's good in bed doesn't mean we should be in a relationship." She glanced up at Cori, suddenly ashen. "I'm sorry, that's so inappropriate."

"Not at all." Cori grinned ear to ear. "But if you don't mind my asking, who are you trying to convince you shouldn't be together? Me or you?"

Nevia took a breath and released it slowly. "I know what I sound like. I sound like a schoolgirl smitten with her first boyfriend. The problem is, I never really did the dating thing in school, and now it just seems so difficult to balance what I want with what he wants. How do people do this? One minute I'm so happy, and I think I might... and then the next I want to stick my gun up his nose."

Cori laughed again. "I'm sorry, Nevia, but that's just how things are sometimes. Don't get me wrong, if he honestly makes you miserable, then you should dump his ass, but if you are struggling to stay away from him, then maybe you should stop struggling, and just be with him."

"I'm not sure if it's my choice anymore. Since yesterday's debacle, he won't talk to me. I think he's coming to the conclusion that I'm not worth the trouble I've gotten him into."

Cori sat up and put her feet on the floor. "Do you love him?"

"I don't know."

"Then decide. Figure it out. If you do love him, then fight for him."

"I'd only be fighting against him," Nevia teased.

"Of course, you need to force him to forgive you, and admit that he's as punch drunk in love with you as you are him."

"How do I even begin to do that?" Nevia's voice rang with defeat even though the battle was just beginning.

"I'm not sure specifically, but I do know it's a precarious balance between patience and persistence. Ethan might have better advice for you." The thought of Ethan made Cori think about her pregnancy. She whipped around and looked at the blood transfusion she was receiving. "Oh, no, did I lose a lot of blood?" She looked back at Nevia.

Nevia nodded, and Cori panicked. She hadn't had much time to get used to the idea of motherhood, but she was certain she didn't want to have a miscarriage.

"It's okay," Nevia said, and Cori ignored her. She frantically waved to get the attention of a nurse. She needed to pee in a cup or something. "The baby is fine," Nevia clarified.

Cori gawked at Nevia, but she remained impassive. "You... knew?"

"If I'm not mistaken, I knew before you did. I congratulated you too soon." Nevia smiled when Cori didn't stop staring. "That was the other reason I hung around. I assumed no one would know to check. The fetus is still alive."

"You can tell all that, just by scent?"

"Pregnancy is fairly easy to detect. Miscarriages also come with signature pheromones. I can even tell you how far along you are." Cori heard a bustle in the nurse's station as Danato entered the infirmary and started yelling and pointing her direction. "Two months," Nevia offered.

Cori gasped and sat back down on the bed. She hadn't assumed she was more than a month. Her calculations must have been very off. Cori heard, more than saw, the parade of nurses rushing toward her room. "Don't tell anyone yet."

"Of course," Nevia said almost scoldingly before the door to Cori's room slammed open, shattering the window in it.

55

S HARDS OF GLASS FELL beside Danato from the door he had just thrown open. Cori jumped and Nevia narrowed her eyes at him. "Clean this up!" he barked at the nurses, who were trailing him to check on Cori. Two jumped back out of the room in search of a dustpan, while the third ran to Cori's side to check her vitals, as he'd *requested*.

"I told you to inform me the minute she was awake." He stared down Nevia, but she didn't flinch. She had an unbreakable quality that made her immune to his anger. That quality, he now knew, was werewolf blood.

"You told me to keep you informed," Nevia clarified. "Had I been given five more minutes to finish my conversation with Cori, I would have contacted you."

"My conversation will be taking precedence."

"Is that before or after you give her a heart attack?" He glowered at her, but she didn't lose stride in her monologue. "I imagine that you would now like to correct me on my conduct, so I will be more than happy to step out into the hall to discuss it with you." Nevia stood and walked out of the room.

Danato looked to Cori, who was nearly catatonic as the nurse made her way through the standard blood pressure, heart, and lung checks. He stepped out into the corridor just as the nurses arrived to clean up the glass.

He watched Cori through the windows while he moved to meet with Nevia. She was waiting patiently a good distance from the room, presumably to mask his yelling, which for the moment was at normal volume. "What?" he asked when he reached her. "I assume that was your way of asking to speak with me alone."

"I thought it necessary to pull you away so you could calm down."

Danato scoffed and looked Nevia over. "You are the strangest cat, aren't you?" he said. "I've never had anyone defy me the way you do, and yet somehow, instead of wanting to rip your head off, I respect you more for it."

"Do you remember the conversation we had about Cori?" Nevia said, ignoring his offhanded compliment. "About you backing her up and supporting her decisions?"

Danato remembered the conversation very clearly. It was one of several conversations in which Nevia had expressed herself to him without restraint. "Yes."

"I would like to amend the advice that I offered you."

"How's that?"

"I've had a little more time to observe you, and I think that your instincts to protect her would be better received at this particular juncture."

Danato smiled and tipped his head to examine her. "You just told me to go easy on her, didn't you?"

"If we must sum it up so plainly, then yes, but more specifically I am suggesting you approach her with the endearment you hold for her on the inside, on the outside, and hide the disappointment and anger about this situation for the time being. I promise you the anger will eventually waver, and you will be glad you took my advice."

Danato narrowed his eyes. "You don't strike me as the type to change your opinion easily. Why are you suddenly more sympathetic to Cori?"

"I'm going to ask for your trust on this. As I've said before, I don't like secrets, but in this particular case, I would like to remain objective rather than truthful."

Danato glanced over at Cori. "Is she okay?" he asked, concerned that Nevia's secret was something health-related.

"Yes," Nevia said simply. "You've calmed enough, I think. If you would like, you could yell at me to maintain face with your employees."

Danato shook his head. "Not necessary. I've already trained them to scatter on approach. Too many bitter years to undo that. You're the only one that I can't quite scare."

"I don't scare easily, warden. If I did, they wouldn't have partnered me with Daniel."

Danato nodded. "We should talk about the Council of the Moon situation before you go. I know I can't offer you much protection, but we should at least come up with a contingency plan if they do come after you."

"Yes, sir." She nodded, and Danato headed back to see Cori.

56

C ORI WAS RELIEVED WHEN Danato left the room. As much as she'd prepared herself to face him over the last two days, it was different in real life. Her potential bravery had shattered right along with the window in the door.

When he came back into the room after his discussion with Nevia, he seemed calmer. But that didn't stop her from cowering like a beaten child. The nurse who had been intently examining her scattered in the wake of his arrival.

"Danato, I..." Her voice croaked again, and she reached for her water glass. It was empty, but Danato came around and refilled it from the plastic pitcher on the bedside table. She looked up at him through her lashes and saw him examining her—his expression yet to be determined. She focused on her water and sipped it carefully. She composed her explanation for her sudden appearance with a gunshot wound to the throat.

Danato sat gingerly on the bed beside her, tapping his cane on his toes before resting it against the bed beside him. He touched her temple to smooth back her hair, and she flinched. When she looked back at him, he looked insulted and hurt, but she couldn't take back the reaction.

She touched the lump of would-be scar on her throat. "Where should I start?" she asked.

He shook his head. "We should wait for Belus for you to report. He's probably not going to be pleased that you missed such an important detail as having a run-in with a genie."

"How did you know?" she asked, neglecting her real question.

"Efrat recalled the incident. *He* seemed to recognize it as something of importance."

She detected a hint of surly sarcasm in that statement, so she didn't bother to ask if *he* was displeased that she missed such an important detail. "I can explain," she said.

"Yes, I'm sure you can," Danato said softly and reached to smooth her hair again. "Are you okay? I mean, aside from the obvious."

"Yes, I'm fine." Cori glanced over to see if Nevia was still there, but she was gone. "Are *you* okay?"

"I'm very angry," he said in his softest voice. "I'm extremely disappointed, but most of all, I'm ashamed." Cori bit back her lips and prepared to hear the speech that had warranted her to make her second wish. "...of myself," Danato added. Her brow dipped in confusion.

Danato rubbed his face before proceeding to explain his sudden change of character. "I was so mad last night.

All I could see were your mistakes, your secrets, and your self-possessed rebellion."

"Now?" Cori prompted when he didn't continue.

"I realize that this is all my fault," he said.

Had she been drinking, Cori would have spat the water out on him. "What?"

"This is why Belus wanted to be in charge of you. He saw this coming. The last two days are a culmination of my double-sided authority. I can't have it both ways."

"But I thought we agreed that you are better as my family than my boss." Cori's eyes were alight with potential tears. Despite what Danato might have thought, the twisted melee of events over the last few days would not have been helped by a heavier hand from him. It was that heavy hand that had prevented her from approaching him to begin with.

"No, I don't mean that. I mean my refusal to share my life with you, and my demand that you tell me everything about yours. I've walled myself up emotionally, and I've walled you in with my protectiveness. I shouldn't have expected you to confide in me when all I do is push and pull you every which way. Your heart must be exhausted from loving and hating me."

Cori's tears shed at the sentiment, and she buried her face in his shoulder. He wrapped his arm around her and rubbed her back soothingly. "Why are you saying all this? You should be yelling until you're red-faced," she mumbled into his shirt.

She could feel him take in a deep breath and let it out slowly. "When that helicopter went down yesterday, I thought you were dead. It almost broke me. It did break Ethan. You are too important to both of us to lose because I can't be level-headed enough to listen when something is wrong. The minute you knew about the elementals, you should have thrown the accusation on my doorstep and demanded an explanation, but I know why you didn't. It pains me greatly that I've built our relationship on love and fear. That's not what I want you to feel toward me."

He scooped her up with no more effort than lifting a child and pulled her into a tighter embrace. She hung her head over his shoulder and cried for what seemed like forever, but it still wasn't long enough.

57

"CORI!" ETHAN HAD NO qualms about stealing her from Danato's grasp, and aside from a trailing grip on her hand, he let him. He embraced her gently, like he might break her, and then he kissed her. The breathtaking kiss made her blush, since it was in the presence of both Danato and Belus.

Belus had trailed in behind Ethan and was leaning against the far wall, not so patiently waiting for the revelries to be over. He was taciturn as usual, but something told her she needed to be careful with how she handled the next few minutes to keep it that way.

Ethan kissed her again, and she pulled away prematurely. "Ethan," she whispered, "we aren't alone."

"I don't care," he whispered back.

She smiled at him warmly and went back to sit on the bed. Danato moved, offering Ethan his position beside her, which he readily took. The last two days—from his perspective—with her in a jail cell and almost getting killed in a helicopter crash—which she barely remembered—had been hard on him. He was only now getting the chance to express his suppressed sentiment.

"Would someone care to update me?" Belus asked disdainfully.

"We were just waiting for you, Belus," Danato said, resting his oversized frame carefully on the aluminum guest chair. "Care to take the lead?"

Belus eyed him suspiciously, but Danato motioned for him to proceed. Cori could see Danato was clenching his jaw, no doubt very literally biting his tongue. Belus paused a good long time just to be sure Danato was giving up the reins before focusing on her.

She straightened up and shrugged off Ethan as nicely as she could. "As you know," she began without further prompting, "during my time-jumping I did have a run-in with a genie. I was not concerned about it, because I was pre-occupied, so in essence, I forgot about it."

"Are you aware of the power that a genie contains?" Belus asked. He was still pretending to be calm and aloof, but Cori could see the ire in his eyes. She wondered if Danato's calm was going to throw imbalance into their good cop, bad cop routine.

"I am now," she stated simply, but with enough force to indicate that further explanation was unnecessary. "Unfortunately, in order to get out of the wishes, I had to negotiate an agreement with him."

"You negotiated with a genie?" Danato said, jolting forward in his chair.

"You and Belus assisted in the negotiations," she reassured him.

"Which did you choose?" Belus asked, concerned.

Cori stopped herself from rolling her eyes at him, which, judging by his expression, was wise. "I, of course, chose the three inconveniences. I could hardly risk anything else." Belus didn't relax at hearing that, but he unclenched his fists, which were balled and white, in order to maintain his reticent behavior.

"I can go into the whole story, but I think we should address my rings first." Everyone perked up. "Thanks to Ethan's assistance, we were able to deduce how the rings were activated." Cori looked at Ethan, who was baffled at her reference to him. She held out her hand. "Take them off."

"I thought they couldn't come off?" he asked, but proceeded to slip one off.

"My dear husband," Cori turned back to address Danato and Belus in turn, "inadvertently spellbound them to protect me with his wedding vows. Since he bound them to me, he is the only one who can take them off."

"Ethan," Belus turned a sharp gaze to him, "take the rest of them off."

Cori's stomach clenched at hearing that statement. It was like the first time they had banned her from her gun. Ethan glanced at Danato for consent and he gave a slight nod. When they were down to the last ring, her wedding ring, he looked up at her for consent. She also gave him a slight nod.

He gathered the rings in his hand and looked at Belus, who was already holding out a small black bag for them. Ethan reluctantly went over and deposited the rings. Belus closed the bag, and it disappeared into one of his pockets.

"We'll explore those later," Belus said to her, either to make her feel better or just to keep her from outright breaking into tears. "Now, what happened after you made your wish?"

58

E THAN LISTENED TO CORI retell her last days, and from what he gathered, it hadn't been much more pleasant than her past few days in this reality. She muddled through her description of her last moments with her mother, but he knew she was only skimming the details so she didn't break down during her recitation of the events.

She explained the immediate suspicion she received from him, Danato, and Belus. She described the strange woman that had taken her place and tried to kill her to prevent her from returning the world to the way it was. She described the resulting fight and final blows. Ethan could tell there was much more to know about her time there, but most of it was probably private and not necessary for her report.

When her summation landed them back in the here and now, Belus looked at Danato. He shrugged. "I'm satisfied if you are."

"Anything else?" Belus asked her.

She cleared her throat. "There were a few strange things about how you and Danato reacted to my presence." Cori looked between the two men, but neither of them reacted to the statement. "I suppose that's not really relevant to my report, though."

"With regard to those many safety protocols that had you being questioned and examined by us in that world," Belus said. "You should know that we aren't any more lenient in this reality. We will require that you stay in the infirmary for another night for tests and observation."

Ethan didn't feel himself standing, but suddenly he was up. Belus eyed him carefully, waiting for the objection. "She is not spending another night in this prison. She has been through enough."

Belus didn't bother to respond. He just stared back at him. It was far more irritating. "Danato?" Ethan looked at his superior, expecting support, but Danato had shifted his gaze to the floor.

"Belus is right. Cori has had interactions with a very powerful being. We should be sure that she is herself before she goes home."

"I told you I would not let her spend one more night in this prison," Ethan bristled, but Cori touched his hand. He looked down at her, and she kissed his palm before cupping it over her cheek.

"It's okay, Ethan. They aren't going to hurt me. You know that. I know that. Belus might ask the nurses to use dull needles, but that's all." She smiled, trying to ease his discontent.

"I just want you safe and sound at home, in my arms," he said.

"That's what Belus is ensuring," she whispered.

Ethan sat back down and slipped his hand into hers. He didn't like being without her, but for some strange reason, everyone had decided to follow the rules for Belus. Considering Ethan was usually the one going by the book, he was wondering what he had missed.

"Oh!" Cori's epiphany startled him. "I have a hole in my brain. Three, actually."

"What?" they all asked simultaneously.

"They did a PET scan and found a few vacancies in my psychic trifecta. Neither of you seemed to know what it was. I thought maybe it might have something to do with the block Cleos put on me."

Danato and Belus exchanged baffled looks. "We'll take another tonight," Belus said. "Hopefully, it was just an anomaly from the rings interfering with the wish. Anything else?"

Cori glanced around at each of them before answering. "There is one more thing."

"There usually is," Belus mumbled.

Cori squeezed Ethan's hand. "When they were doing the tests, they found something else." The somber tone in her voice made his heart clench. His first thought was Cori's family history of cancer. "I guess... I'm pregnant."

He exhaled, trying to find the right reaction to the sentiment he was feeling. For a moment, he just stared blankly at her. Her face soured, and she drew her hand away from his. He glanced at Danato for his reaction, and he found the man beaming. Had Ethan not been in his way, he was certain he would have already scooped Cori up in his arms and spun her around. Belus even had a smile on his face that he was doing his best to hide.

"Ethan," Danato shook him from his vacuous thoughts. "Say something."

Ethan looked back at Cori. She looked shattered by his non-reaction. He couldn't muster the strength to stand and twirl her as Danato would in countless seconds. All he could do was slip off the bed to his knees and bury his face in her lap.

Cori naturally petted his head, and when he looked at her through stinging eyes, she frowned. "Tell me this makes you happy," Ethan said, drawing her hands to his lips to kiss them.

"Yes," she stated with a small smile, not unlike Belus's.

He touched her belly, but so far, nothing was different. A thought occurred to him and he stood up. "We need to check the baby! You lost a lot of blood, plus the trauma!"

"The baby is fine." Cori stood and pressed her hands to his shoulders. "Nevia confirmed that I'm about two months along. I trust her."

He calmed considerably, since he also trusted Nevia, but he now had a new number in mind. Not nine months, but seven. In just over two seasons, he was going to be a father. "Belus!" Ethan cornered him before he could escape the festivities. "We need to warn the nurses. She's going to need an ultrasound and those pre-natal vitamins."

"Easy, sport," Belus said. "Let's just get through one day without panic, shall we?"

"But we aren't prepared for a baby."

Belus smirked. "Speak for yourself." He nodded back to Danato, who had finally scooped Cori up into his arms.

Ethan watched the burly man weep over the news just as he had a moment ago. He assumed it was all from joy, but when he nearly dropped Cori and reached for his cane, he thought otherwise.

"Danato!" Ethan rushed over to help him. "What is it?"

"Too long of a night," he said, waving him and Cori away. "I should get home and rest. You two probably want some time together. Belus will hold off on the tests until later." Belus gave a disinterested nod and held the door open for Danato to pass through.

When they were gone, Ethan kissed Cori the way he'd wanted to from the moment he had walked into the room.

59

DANATO RESTED AGAINST THE glass wall near the nurse's station while Belus found a nurse to help him. He returned with a large-chested, giggling blonde. She eyed Danato woefully before raising her needle and instructing him to lower his trousers. With a quick swab of alcohol, a prick of the needle, and a wink for Belus, she was back to her work in one of the labs.

"Why do you get all the winks?" Danato grumbled as he tried to walk again.

"Because I'm reliable and funny."

"I don't remember you ever being funny." Danato smirked at him.

"That's because you have no sense of humor." Belus smirked back. "How are you doing?"

"It's coming along. You mind walking me home?"

"That bad?" Belus stopped in his tracks. If Danato gave the word, he would call the nurse to bring him a wheelchair.

"No. I mean yes, but... I thought we could have a drink." Danato wasn't sure what thought had passed through Belus's mind at that moment, but he could have guessed. The discomfort was there and gone. "Unless you promised that voluptuous young woman your time," Danato added, in case he wanted to make an excuse to get out of it.

Belus glanced back at the door the nurse had disappeared through. "She'll keep. We should probably talk about what just happened in there, anyway."

"Which part?" Danato raised his brow.

Belus scoffed. "Take your pick. Fuck, she's a pain in the ass."

Danato couldn't help laughing, but only because he knew Belus was just as fond of Cori as he was.

Once they reached the house, Danato let Belus pick the liquor, in part because he didn't want to move from his chair. Belus stood in front of the cupboard for a long time before he pulled out a cognac that was half gone. He recognized it instantly.

Belus paused, holding it in view, as if he were waiting for an objection. When Danato didn't give one, Belus poured a shot's worth for each of them. They raised the glasses and clinked them. Neither of them offered a toast, but they already knew what they were drinking to.

After they each gulped down the liquor, Belus put the bottle back and pulled out a less expensive bottle of rum. He poured them each a half glass and settled himself on the couch to sip the drink.

Danato imagined that he might have stayed silent for hours if he didn't have so much on his mind to discuss.

As it was, it took nearly three minutes for him to speak. "What was that back there?"

"Care to be more specific?" Danato asked, poking his cane at a fallen log in the fire.

"The part where you just threw the reins at me."

"Cori is your responsibility now, isn't that what we decided?"

"Yes, that's what we decided, but we both know that you were never comfortable with that arrangement. It's unfair to Cori to be bounced around like this: me to you, good guy you to bad guy you, and back to me again. She isn't a natural soldier like Ethan."

"I agree. That's why I'm giving you the reins, or giving you *back* the reins. I'm done trying to be her slaver and her savior."

"We've had this conversation before, Danato. What's different this time around?"

"A lot and nothing. I walked into that room today with a measure of control over my anger, per Jordan's request. Which I'm glad she made, since Cori is likely to think twice about raising a child around a cantankerous ill-tempered old man." Danato smiled, again thinking about a baby coming into the house. "I sat down next to her to talk. I moved my hand to brush her hair from her face, and she recoiled."

Danato took a drink and thought about that moment, and how offended and hurt he'd been by her reaction.

Since it was an honest reflex, he only had himself to blame for losing her trust.

"I don't want to be that man, Belus," Danato mumbled, staring into the fire. "I don't know where it all went wrong... I mean... I do, but..."

"Cori's been through a lot the past couple of days," Belus offered.

"I would never hurt her. As angry as I've ever been, I would break my own hand before I would allow that."

"She knows that."

"No, she *knew* that, but everything has gotten confused."

"She is still to blame for a good amount of that confusion," Belus pointed out.

"Yes, but I am to blame for her. I'm not saying you shouldn't do as you see fit to amend her... character flaws, but I am saying that you should bear in mind that I let things get this far, and it's not her fault that I lost focus with her the minute she was no longer going to be my successor."

Belus poured himself another quarter glass of rum and leaned over his knees on the couch, examining the liquor. "We've got seven very long months ahead of us: elementals, baby-proofing, and trying to avoid an audit—which is most likely unavoidable," Belus grumbled.

Danato nodded.

"I'd better get back in there before Ethan tries to break her out. I'm starting to think you're relinquishing your authority just to ease your workload."

Danato smiled broadly. "Damn right. I've got to make myself available to babysit."

Belus chuckled and swallowed down his drink. "You need anything?" He motioned to his leg, but Danato shook his head. "You know it's only going to get worse."

"It'll be worth it."

"If you say so." Belus looked down at his leg. "I'm not sure a wheelchair isn't in your future seven months from now."

"It'll still be worth it," Danato reiterated. Belus may not have agreed, but there wasn't much he could do about it. By this point, the only hope to reduce the pain in his leg was amputation, and he wasn't that desperate yet.

60

Cori jerked up from her hospital bed, gasping for air and clasping at her throat. "Easy, kid," she heard from the corner of the darkened room.

"Belus?" She focused on his shadow as her eyes adjusted to the night lighting in the infirmary. There was a distant light at the nurse's terminal, but otherwise it was dark.

"Nightmares?" he asked, moving over to the bed.

She nodded, covering her face. "Fresh ones." The words came out muffled, but she didn't move her hands. She could feel him sit down on the bed next to her. "I'm okay," she said, sniffling.

"Sure, kid." He tugged back her hands, and she rested them on her lap. "You want to talk about it? Sometimes it loosens the dream-feeders' grip."

"I killed her, Belus," she said, wiping away her tears. "I've never intentionally killed anyone, but she killed you and she was killing me, so I stabbed her."

"Yeah, you always do get bent out of shape when someone kills me."

"It's not funny, Belus." She pulled her blanket back up to cover her. "What are you doing here? It's the middle of the night."

"Checking in on you."

"You should be sleeping. Sleep is good when you can get it." Cori yawned and rolled over, and huddled into her blankets. Her eyes dropped shut, but Belus didn't get the hint.

"Your tests came back. The scan showed a deprivation of activity in your psychic brain centers, just like you said."

"Yeah, see? Holes."

"You think Cleos did something to cause this?"

"I don't know, but I can't ask him cause he hates me right now."

She could hear him exhale with exasperation. "Why does he hate you?"

"Because I forgave him for lob—erasing those women."

"Why would you forgive him for that? He erased their existence."

"Because they asked him to do it. They were on the verge of suicide. He tried to remove some of the bad memories, but it didn't work. Too many bad memories. He didn't want them to die, so he offered them a new life. A real new life, without all the bad. He wasn't doing it to feed on them. He was doing it to save their lives. I forgave him. Apparently, I insulted his pride. Now he hates me."

"Cori, are you sure about that? Did he admit that to you?"

"Admit that he hates me? It was obvious."

"No, did he tell you those women asked to be erased?"

"No, I heard it for myself, in his mind." She could practically see the cogs in his brain turning, but he asked nothing else. He shifted off the bed. "Belus?"

"What, Cori?"

"You didn't seem very happy about the baby."

"Oh, no?" He pretended to have no idea what she was talking about, but she heard the humor in his tone.

"Not unhappy, just not very happy."

"Well," he returned to the bed. "I imagine I'm about as happy as you are." She opened her eyes, prepared to defend herself, but Belus's simper told her he wasn't trying to insult her. "I imagine you're excited and yet terrified about raising a child here. That's where I am right now. However, to answer the question you didn't actually ask: yes, I am happy that you're pregnant."

Cori was relieved she was not the only one concerned about the future. "How *do* I raise a child here, Belus? How will I protect it? What about school and friends? There are no other children here to play with." Cori could feel herself panicking, but she couldn't stop thinking about the questions Gypsy had posed to her.

"Cori, relax. The baby will be safe. We will all protect it. We will utilize tutors and private schooling. There are no children here to play with because this is a prison, and to some extent that will never change, but obviously with time, leniencies will be made. You are not alone in balancing this lifestyle with children. Many of our recruited staff have families that they only see quarterly during their term."

"Are you saying I have to ship my child to boarding school?"

Belus smirked. "I'm saying decisions will have to be made that will both benefit the child and protect the prison, regardless of how hard it is on your maternal instincts."

Cori grimaced, but she knew that there was bound to be a price for raising a child here. She was thinking it would be the lack of cable television and music, but apparently there were worse things in life.

Belus touched her shoulder and headed to the door. When his hand was on the doorknob, she found her voice again. "Belus." He paused at the door, not taking his hand off the handle. "Can I ask you another question?"

"Only if you tell me why you waited for me to get all the way to the door to ask."

"Cause that's how long it took me to find my nerve." She sat up against her pillows, pulling her knees in tight.

Belus observed the change and came back over to hear her out. "What is it?"

She cleared her throat, which made it hurt, so she reached for more water. After a sip, she held the water between her hands and knees, mostly to have something to do with her hands. "I said before that you and Danato acted strangely when I got to the prison to fix my wishes. Danato took one look at me and kissed me, and not really in a nice-to-meet-you way. More like a thank-God-you're-home kind of way."

"Danato has a lot of Italian roots. Kissing is a lot like shaking hands for them."

"I thought *that* was strange, until you got involved," she said, ignoring his levity. "You almost shot me at first sight." Belus's jaw clenched, and she waited for him to respond, but he didn't. "You were not happy to make my acquaintance, and I asked you why. You told me that I looked like Olivia. I know that she was Danato's wife, and I know that she is deceased, and you have alluded to her being the reason your relationship with Danato has been precarious. However, what I don't understand is why when you are suddenly faced with a woman that looks just like your friend's dead wife, that you would consider shooting first and asking questions later."

"Last night, with Efrat, was the first time I've touched a pistol in years." Belus stepped over to her and took the glass from her hands to set it on the nightstand. He lifted her blankets and ushered her to sink into them. As she did, she noticed his glassy eyes frozen at the onset of anguish.

"Why would seeing Olivia again prompt you to change that?" she asked as he pulled the covers to her neck.

"Because the last time I held a gun in my hand was to shoot her." His voice strained to a whisper.

Cori stared blankly at him. "Belus..."

She didn't know what to say to him, but his fingers pressed to her lips, interrupting her attempt. She could feel his hand shaking as he moved it to her cheek and gently caressed it with his thumb. "That's enough for tonight," he whispered.

She nodded slightly. He pulled away, leaving her bereft of contact and alone to contemplate what possible scenario could have forced the usually level-headed Belus to kill Danato's wife.

FELICIA
JEDLICKA
BEASTS
&
BURDENS
BOOK 8
THE WARDEN

BEASTS &
BURDENS

Sneak Peek

CORI GASPED AT THE feeling of her stomach going into her throat. The roar of metal grinding on metal screamed all around her. The flickering lights added to the horror-movie feel. She wanted to scream, because she knew in mere seconds she was going to be dead, but nothing came out.

Efrat lassoed his arm around her back and pulled her impermissibly to him. "Grab onto me!" he yelled into her ear over the noise.

She hooked her arms around his neck while he extended his arms toward the adjacent walls. She felt the tingle of electric blue and she buried her face into his neck.

They both lifted from the floor, held up by Efrat's magnetism. His knees lifted beneath her, cradling her further. She could feel his heart racing and his ragged breathing from the effort.

The noise crested with the elevator landing in the sub-basement. Efrat's energy fluctuated, and they landed on the splintered floor of the elevator. He absorbed most of the impact, as she was essentially still in his lap.

She listened to him pant, but didn't bother to look up at him. She wanted to cry, and she was pretty sure that it wasn't just her hormones talking. She had not been this certain of her death since she fell off the roof.

Some part of her was shaking—it could have been all of her. Efrat wrapped his arms around her, pressing his hands flat against her back. Since she wasn't getting shocked, she didn't try to stop him.

They stayed like that for several seconds, possibly even a minute. Cori was about to collect herself and pull away from him when the elevator door ripped off with a horrific squeal that made her jump. She looked up and saw Danato, along with several guards, peering into the half-lit elevator. His eyes widened at the scene he witnessed.

Thank you so much for reading. I hope you enjoyed the ride and if you aren't getting off here, I encourage you to sign up for my newsletter so I can return your generosity with new release updates and special offers.

Sign-Up

You can also find me on Facebook or visit my website. Keep reading!

Website

Facebook

AUTHOR

As a Nebraska native, and a small-town girl at that, I have very little to occupy my time beyond imagining a world outside of my own reality. By the grace of God and the seat of my pants, I have kept my waning attention span on the task of becoming an author.

So here I am, an indie author, peddling my words in cyberspace and enduring my comeuppances with an unwavering determination. I may not be a professional, and I certainly am not perfect, but if you've made it this far, you have to admit, this smartass yokel does spin quite a yarn.

From the self-inflicted sweatshop conditions of my unairconditioned childhood home, to the arthritis reaping positions of a sedentary lifestyle, I bring to you: my sarcasm, my oddity, and my heart. Take it with a grain of salt or a teaspoon of sugar, but take it for what it is: a story born of the mind, translated to paper, and gifted to you.

I thank you for your readership and even more for your support. Please recommend this book to your friends and family via any social media that you use. Word of mouth is still the best advertising and is greatly appreciated.

Most importantly, keep reading. I'll keep writing.

www.ingramcontent.com/pod-product-compliance
Lightning Source LLC
Chambersburg PA
CBHW011437200726
48289CB00009BA/2793